Jan Stechpalm
Odyssey through Russia

AF190172

Jan Stechpalm

Odyssey through Russia

Dieter Hüllstrung's Experiences

on the Eastern Front and in Captivity

1945–1949

BoD-Verlag

Norderstedt

2019

Bibliografische Information der Deutschen Nationalbibliothek:
Die Deutsche Nationalbibliothek verzeichnet diese Publikation in der Deutschen Nationalbibliografie; detaillierte bibliografische Daten sind im Internet über www.dnb.de abrufbar.
Bibliographic Information of the German National Library:
The German National Library lists this publication in the German National Bibliography; detailed bibliographic data can be found under www.dnb.de.

Impressum
© 2019 Jan D. Stechpalm
The Original German Edition
Odyssee durch Russland
was published by Literareon in:
Herbert Utz Verlag, München 2011

Translation: Andrea Dannegger
Proofreading: Julia Koppitz
Cover design: Jan D. Stechpalm
Set & Layout: Jan D. Stechpalm

Production & Edition: BoD - Books on Demand, Norderstedt
ISBN: 9-7837481-82382

Cover: Tobacco case with leather bag made by Dieter Hüllstrung during his captivity in a Russian POW camp. Inside the case: Dieter Hüllstrung's Russian ticket out of prison and cigarette paper.

Table of Contents

Introduction

As a young boy I always loved it when my father recited classical theatre dialogues, dramatic ballads or when he read adventure stories to us. He managed to make the scenes come alive so well by changing his voice, facial expressions, the pace of his reading and had us completely captivated by the fiery sparkle in his eyes. This filled the long, late and cosy evenings of our skiing holidays in the Swiss Alps or at home, when guests from distant countries filled the vaulted living room of our turn-of-the-century townhouse and curious neighbours came by to listen to my father's stories, ask his advice or learn something about Latin, theology, philosophy or history – all obsessions of his.

At first, when I was younger, I romanticised his World War II stories as one might a wild west novel or a pirate tale. In fact, my father was sent to serve at the Russian front where, at the age of 19, he was captured and spent five long years of his youth in Russian captivity. As I grew older, new facets of his experiences began to interest me: How could anyone even survive such an ordeal? What survival skills and tricks had my father developed? How had he experienced Germany's defeat? How had he overcome the brutalities of war? Had he been able to find any joys during this time? Had he ever killed anyone?

Unfortunately, before his death in the year 2000, my father had not heeded my request to write down these experiences for his children and grandchildren, as his own father had done with his memoirs of World War I. However, in the spring of 2000, as if with a sense of foreboding, we sat together in the evenings of our last skiing holiday in the Swiss Alps and scribbled down dates and places of his captivity on a few sheets of paper.

I was left with these sketchy notes, his photo album, my memories of his telling, audio tapes of his evening stories and his correspondence with his parents during his captivity. Armed with these, as well as my own painstaking research in books and on the Internet, I began the attempt of weaving these threads into his story.

If one examines the history around the collapse of the Eastern Front, the 'Heeresgruppe Mitte', and around German prisoners of war (POWs) in Russia during and after World War II, one will find a great deal of literature on the subject. My research began with the 15-volume work *The History of German Prisoners of War in the Second World War* (*Zur Geschichte der deutschen Kriegsgefangenen des Zweiten Weltkrieges*) by E. Maschke. In 1957, Maschke had founded the 'Scientific Commission for the History of the German Prisoners of War' to investigate the atrocities against German POWs. The committee compiled a wealth of data, researching field posts, reports by returnees and the documents of non-profit organizations, such as the Red Cross, among others.

After the end of the Cold War in the early 1990s, the Soviet archives were gradually opened for research, among them the Central Archive of the Russian Federation, as well as many local archives in the respective regions of the prison camps. This also included the headquarters for storing historical and documentary collections with over two million detainee records, pay-books, letters and photographs of German POWs. An in-depth historical overview can be found in more recent books, such as *In the GUPVI Archipelago, Prisoners of War in the Soviet Union, 1941–1956* (*Im Archipel GUPVI, Kriegsgefangenschaft in der Sowjetunion 1941–1956*) by S. Karner (1995) or *German POWs in the Soviet Union, 1941–1956; POW Policy, Camp Life and Memories* (*Deutsche Kriegsgefangene in der Sowjetunion, 1941–1956; Kriegsge-*

fangenenpolitik, Lageralltag und Erinnerungen) by A. Hilger (2000). Interesting published reports of individual stories can also be found in the German authors' book series *Storytelling is Remembering* (*Erzählen ist Erinnern*) of the German war graves commission ('Volksbund Deutsche Kriegsgräberfürsorge e.V.'), for example, in Volume 27, 'Resisting or adapting? A question of Survival' (*Anpassen oder Widerstehen? Eine Überlebensfrage*) by J. Wildenhain or in Volume 30, 'Forty-nine Months. Russian War Imprisonment from May 1945 to June 1949' (*Neunundvierzig Monate. In russischer Kriegsgefangenschaft Mai 1945 bis Juni 1949*) by E. Eicher.

While researching the background information, contradictory statements by various authors were uncovered, especially when it came to estimates of troop sizes, the number of prisoners and the number of dead. Furthermore, I discovered contradictions and haziness concerning my father's personal fate within my own sources.

The content of this book can, therefore, best be seen as an approximation of the actual course of events. The language in places may seem somewhat colloquial. This tone was used deliberately to lend authenticity to the experiences of the young soldier that Dieter was. Ultimately, it was not my ambition to reproduce this complex part of history in a scientifically exact historical-critical manner on paper. This has already been accomplished by much better-skilled authors. The driving force behind this exciting venture was simply that this extraordinary chapter in my father's life should not be forgotten by our own family and for generations to come. If it succeeds in enticing you, the reader, to reflect on your own heritage, your values, on the necessary and the superfluous as well as on the enduring and the transient aspects of life, then the effort was more than worthwhile.

Jan D. Stechpalm

Dieter Hüllstrung
(*1925 - †2000)

Odyssey to the Eastern Front

He sat in the train from Warsaw to Moscow somewhere between Brest and Minsk. A landscape of wooded hills and cultivated fields slid by before his eyes and let his mind drift back home to Karlsruhe and to the northern Black Forest, where he had spent his childhood and youth in similar hills. In summer times he had loved exploring woods and hills like those by long cycling tours and hikes. He had set with friends around campfires for endless evenings. Their songs resonated in his ears.

Suddenly there was a violent jolt and the sounds of the screeching brakes. The train stopped abruptly in the middle of the forest. Someone shouted: 'Air raid! Everyone out of the train!' Panic ensued, as the soldiers grabbed their weapons, rushed out of the railcars and ran at lightning speed down the railway embankment to find cover in the woods. Overhead, several Russian combat planes dived like buzzards towards the train. The howling engines and salvos of machinegun fire filled the air, before they disappeared in the grey of the sky again.

For the first time in his life, Dieter felt a real fear for his life. This was not how he had imagined things would be. He was only 19 years old and on his way to join the Second World War, on his way to the Eastern Front. Everyone training to become an officer had to serve at least three months at the front. Just one year before, in March 1943, he had received his high school diploma. He was still half a boy, a late bloomer. So far, he had not even needed to shave. His graduating class had only consisted of seven boys. The older ones, born in 1924 – there had been twenty-four – had graduated from high school a quarter of a year earlier and had been 'allowed' to enrol for military service. The boys were taught to believe that the path of a soldier to war was a favourable opportunity to achieve fame and honour for the '*Führer*', the '*Volk*' and the '*Vaterland*'. Two or three had died in their first few days at the front. By the end of the war only 20 of the 30 boys would survive. So much for the 'privilege' of going to war for 'leader, folk and country'!

The Reich Labour Service and Basic Military Training

On 17 April 1943, Dieter had to leave home to serve in the obligatory labour service of the Third Reich, something every youth had to complete before his military service. Dieter was called in to Landau, Pfalz. There, for a short time, he found pleasant companions. He was also promoted several times: on 16 June to Foreman and on 8 July to Chief Foreman. Unfortunately, this promising start to a heroic military career was thwarted by scarlet fever. For three weeks, sick with fever and a scalding throat, he felt the fallibility of his limbs. The only thing *he* was guarding was his bed, while others pursued the highest, unspoiled dreams of youth to become daring soldiers. Could this have been a warning of the suffering that awaited him at war?

Photo: Dieter at the Reich Labour Service
in Landau (second from right)

In mid-July 1943, Dieter was finally able to enroll for basic military training with the 5th Artillery Regiment in Ulm.

There, his training as a gunner on the light field howitzer (LFH 16) began. This artillery gun (pictured below) had a caliber of 10.5 cm (4.13 inches) and ran with two spare carriages. It weighed 1,525 kg (3,362 lbs), was 5 m (16.5 ft) long, 1.65 meters (5.5 ft) high and carried the shot at an exit velocity of about 470 m/s (1,542 ft/s) with a maximum firing range of 10,675 m (11,675 yds). As a gunner, Dieter was the soldier who had to calculate the launch angle and launch direction and then make adjustments according to the reported hit. The other shooters on the howitzer had to launch the shot, if necessary change the position of the gun and load new ammunition into the howitzer.[1]

Light Field Howitzer 16 on carriage

The basic training consisted first of the drill in the combat formation, of long marches with heavy baggage in rank and file, the use of rifle and handgun, setting up and dismantling field camps, digging safety trenches, creating camouflage and last but not least, learning the indispensable and, later

[1] Panzermuseum Münster, http://www.panzermuseum.com/

at the front, what would prove life-saving, measure of military discipline. This had been drummed into them by sharp, seemingly pitiless officers and sergeants, who like vicious shepherd dogs wandered constantly around the flock, barking faulty recruits back into line or penalising them with extra laps.

In addition, Dieter also learned the technical skills required to operate and maintain an artillery gun. This he found very enjoyable, because the mathematics used to calculate the ballistic trajectories of projectiles came easily to him. In the middle of this rather mindless military life, where unreflective, gear-like operation was more important than independent thinking, it gave him the feeling that he still belonged to an intelligent species.

After a mere two weeks, he was sent to the Reserve Officer Applicant (*Reserveoffiziersbewerber*), or in short, 'ROB'-course, to Dijon, where he spent six months and where, in addition to mathematical and technical skills, he learned lessons in military leadership and tactics. The army was now in a hurry to train new soldiers for the front. Up to this point, everything had had a rather sporting-fellowship character; in Dijon, he had even won a shooting competition as the gunner of his howitzer. The camaraderie reminded him of his time in the German Youth and Hitler Youth[2], the obligatory youth organisations of the Nazi Party.

Then things became more serious.

At morning roll call on 3 January 1944, his division was given the transfer order. However, because he had severely chafed his instep during his last practice march, the barracks

---

[2] From 1933 until 1945, there was only one official youth organisation in Germany, as organised by the Nazi Party (NSDAP). Every 10–13-year-old boy was required to join the 'German Youth' (*Deutsches Jungvolk*) and 14–18-year-olds joined the 'Hitler Youth' proper (*Hitlerjugend*). Dieter served as violinist in the 'Bann'-Orchestra of the Hitler Youth, travelling to concerts throughout Baden.

doctor found him 'unfit to march', and he had to stay behind at the general hospital in Dijon, while his comrades were sent towards the 'enemy'. For Dieter, this meant three weeks of strict bed rest with a plaster cast. He was placed in the ward for skin and venereal diseases, where – in his youthful innocence – his greatest fear was of catching a 'nasty' disease. Luckily, he had found an original version of Goethe's *Faust* in a bookshop during one of the outings in the French old-town of Dijon. This cheered him up.

Finally, he was released from hospital, still limping. From the command post, he found out where his 'pack' had landed: on the island of Walcheren at Westkapelle, just off the Dutch North Sea coast. They had been selected to confront the anticipated sea invasion of the '*Tommies*', their name for the Englishmen. To Dieter that certainly sounded heroic. Now he would surely be able to complete his ROB-course.

First Deployment to Walcheren

The voyage to Walcheren was an adventure. Dieter travelled in trains crowded with soldiers with all of his gear via Paris, Brussels and Amsterdam. Every train station was teeming with dense crowds of German soldiers, through which Dieter, with his injured foot and heavy baggage, had to struggle. At every station he panicked that he might miss his connecting train. In Paris, however, he took advantage of a longer stopover for a trip on the subway, the famous 'Metro' – one last encounter with civilian life. The time had flown by.

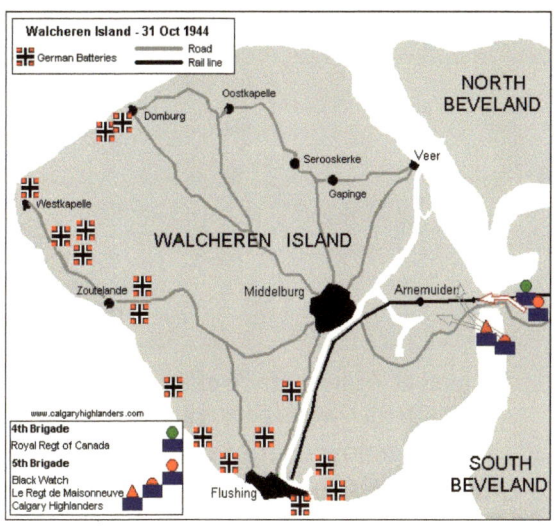

Walcheren Island in 1944
http://upload.wikimedia.org/wikipedia/commons/
d/d4/Walcheren2.gif

On the island of Walcheren, Dieter was first positioned in Westkapelle on the howitzer as a gunner. This did not appeal to him because of the four comrades on the gun, three were incompetent. They did not cooperate properly with the team and, instead, looked after themselves. He was very happy, therefore, when, on his 19th birthday, on 19 February 1944,

17

he was transferred as assistant observer to the observation post of the battery. There he found himself in a downright homely bunker with a ventilation system and a tank dome directly on top of the dunes. The constant sound of the wind and waves gave him a feeling of immediacy to life and of an uninterrupted world order. Unfortunately, after a few days they were moved from there to another temporary observation post, which was a former Dutch artillery bunker: cold, cramped and dirty, but still close to the sea.

Bunker at Zoutelande, Walcheren, 1943
(from Dieter's photo album)

Dieter had greatly enjoyed the sea and the thundering waves. He often walked alone down to the breakwaters to read his *Faust*, or just to feel the wind and water spray on his skin.

His next posting in wait for the *'Tommies'* was two kilometres from the sea and was once again a little more habitable. It was in a lighthouse where Dieter had a view around the island and, of course, over the English Channel, from where the enemy was expected to come. In good weather he could see the Dutch mainland and the estuary of the river Schelde. From there, on 8 March 1944, he wrote a letter to his dancing class partner, Marlene, who, at that time, was just finishing high school. He told her about Dijon and Walcheren and the soldier's life:

'[...] the "Kommiss" [military life] doesn't hold a candle to civilian [life]. The only enjoyable events are ordinary benders, which, incidentally, I have also participated in (last night, three of us "finished off" a one-litre bottle of cognac. There was a kind of a burnt punch: one lights the liquor on fire and holds sugar cubes with a fork over the alcohol flame, which then melts and crashes sizzling into the brew.) I would not recommend it to you, as it is rather something for tough warriors (a year ago I would not have dared to drink it). We call it Krambambuli and prepare it as if it were a sacred ceremony. But this is the only joy, I should write fun, because the other pleasures are not pure. If I pick up Faust *in the evening, just to read it, someone will surely start whistling a rhythmic Fox or something else I love so much. I'm outright hungry for good music, after respectable entertainment, in general for the way of life that I am used to. [...]'* [3]

Yes, the young soldiers drank for courage in the war, although the only people they encountered were the voluptuous, native Dutch women in their traditional costumes and wooden shoes, and still the enemy kept them waiting.

Before his 'real' entry into this war, Dieter had a layover in Strasbourg from Easter to June 1944. He had been transferred to the heavy weapons unit of the Artillery Regiment 213 with thirty other ROBs, to the barracks in Neudorf-Süd, a suburb of Strasbourg. During a training manoeuvre in Münsingen he was promoted to corporal and assistant instructor. It was there that they experienced – as a kind of foretaste of the war – the air raid on Strasbourg. And finally, during a

---

[3] Hüllstrung, D., Letter to Marlene, dated 8 March 1944

home leave in Karlsruhe, he had been able to see his parents for what would be the last time in a long while.

Dieter (right) with his brother Wolfgang
in 1942

In the expectation of a quick return home, Dieter enrolled at the Technical University of Karlsruhe as a student. After all, the war could not last forever, could it? And he already had his goal in mind: he wanted to become a chemist. His mother was worried because now the last of her three men had gone to war. His older brother Wolfgang had sent his last field letter in 1942 from Stalingrad and hadn't been heard from since. His father, Kurt was only home on a short leave and had to return to Sicily soon, where he was Captain of a staff unit for Rommel's *'Heeresstreife Africa'*.

Dieter (right) with his father Capt. Kurt
Hüllstrung in 1944

On 22 June 1944, all ROBs were finally set in motion again, each sent to another unit. Dieter, together with four other ROBs, had received the marching order: 'Bobruisk'. So, together with Hildebrandt, Wöhrle, Frank and another comrade, the odyssey to the 35th Artillery Regiment of the 35th Infantry Division (= 'Fish Division') under Lieutenant General J.-G. Richert had begun. They travelled by train via Frankfurt, Dresden and Warsaw. On 23 June 1944, at a stop in Brest, they noticed a train on the opposite track of the platform, which carried soldiers returning home on leave. Dieter could not read much more than fatigue and war weariness on their faces, especially since the depressing news of D-Day had made its sobering rounds: the landing of the so-called Allies[4] on 20 June 1944 in Normandy.

---

[4] The Allies = the anti-German coalition (here referring primarily to Great Britain, France, Russia and the USA).

The Madman Adolf's War World

The five companions did not have the slightest idea of the mess they were heading into. The war was in its fifth year and was long lost before they were even drafted. Eleven years earlier, in 1933, Adolf Hitler had come to power in Germany. Although he was elected freely by the people to be their democratic Chancellor, he transformed the democratic constitution of Germany quickly in order to become the sole, undisputed ruler of Germany: a ruthless dictator, the 'Führer' (leader) – as he wanted to be called. From then on, he could not be halted to pursue only his own goals with all his might. Anyone who opposed his will was imprisoned or killed. His objectives were to wage a war to conquer Europe and to force it together into one empire which should last for a thousand years: the so-called 'Reich'. After six years under his rule, Germany had already reached Hitler's first insane goal: war. At first, it even seemed as if the second goal would be attained as quickly: the conquest of Europe. In 1938, Austria was 'absorbed' into Hitler's Reich with very little resistance. The logic was simple since, at the end of the First World War in 1918, this unification had already been agreed upon by the Austrian National Assembly of the time, but the winning war powers of the First World War (Britain, France, the USA and Russia) had opposed and prevented it from being realised. In addition, Hitler had a personal reason for this annexation: he was born and brought up in Austria.

Austria was followed by Czechoslovakia in 1939. Afterwards, the brave German soldiers under their maniacal leader conquered one country after another during the early years of the war: Poland, Denmark, Norway, Belgium, Holland and part of France. They marched through Hungary, Romania, Bulgaria and Finland. Yes, the German armies invaded

Greece, Morocco and Algeria and even reached Egypt. But like Caesar and Napoleon before him, the more Hitler conquered and controlled the more control he wanted.

Many have tried to understand the phenomenon of insatiable powerholders and explained it by the corrupt forces, which inhabit power and to which weak personalities can't resist. In Hitler's case, it would be too simple to assume, that he was only corrupted or addicted to power like the notorious drinker, which falls for the ease and sensual smoothening of his drug. No, Hitler must have seen himself confirmed in his deranged beliefs of 'Arian' supremacy by the course of the events. This belief in supremacy is based on the right of the stronger. This belief gave the winner the 'right' and the looser the 'wrong'. Hitler had derived his insane concept of the world amongst others from the writings of Darwin, Galton and Nietzsche. The first, Charles Darwin, had described the 'survival of the fittest' as a law of nature, which could possibly explain the evolution of life on Earth. The second, Darwin's cousin Francis Galton, had transferred this theory to a concept of society, nowadays called 'social Darwinism', according to which societies could only survive, if they'd be fitter than other societies. This had given ground to the immoral concept of 'racial hygiene', the distorted views, that a race became fitter, by killing the weak and sick and by breeding the strongest and fittest humans like race horses. The third, Friedrich Nietzsche, was an incredibly sharp and deep thinker of the turn of the century, who in a time of unprecedented new scientific understandings about life on Earth and elevating technological advances, had tried to found a new system of values. After the falls of millenniums of royal and religious powers and their authorizations through dogmatic beliefs in their values, which had been slowly eroded by those leaders, as they stopped following their own moral, so that they were set out of power by their slowly through rational enlightenment matured, liberated and self-empowered citizen. Unfortunately, Hitler's humanity-defying supremacist views still find followers in our days.

Hitler's next target was Russia and therefore, with 'Operation Barbarossa', he sent an army of roughly seven million men under the command of General Field Marshal von Brauchitsch towards the east.

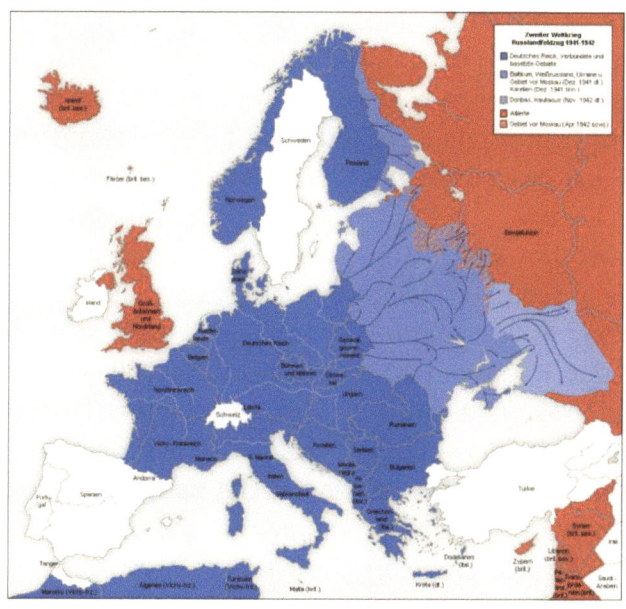

Germany 1941
http://commons.wikimedia.org/wiki/File:Second_world_
war_europe_1941-1942_map_de.png

The Russian Campaign

Hitler's Russian war campaign, 'Operation Barbarossa', was launched on 22 June 1941. The German armies pushed into the East in three groups. The Army Group North ran through the Baltic countries against Leningrad, the Army Group Center pulled through East Prussia against Minsk, Smolensk and Moscow and the Army Group South cut through the Ukraine towards Southern Russia. Still today, estimates regarding the balance of power in this war campaign differ widely, depending on the political affiliation of the historian. In any case, several million soldiers, thousands of tanks and thousands of fighter jets were found on both sides of the frontline. It was one of the most powerful and violent conflicts in human history.

On 2 October 1941, German troops had advanced to just outside of Moscow and began their attack on the Soviet capital known as 'Operation Typhoon'. Until then, approximately 200,000 Russians had been killed, 700,000 were injured and 200,000 were missing, while the German losses were allegedly still relatively low. The tank units rolled within 30 kilometres of Moscow. However, the opposition grew, and then Russia's greatest ally stepped in, the one who had already defeated Napoleon all of those years ago: the deep Russian winter. By the end of November, temperatures on the eastern front had dropped to -25 degrees Celsius (-13 F) and lower.

In the midst of it all stood Karl Ernst, Dieter's cousin, an officer-in-training in a pioneer troop section. He remembered how they had tried to protect themselves by every imaginable means against icy, biting temperatures reaching -45°C (-49°F). Like Napoleon before them, the German Armed Forces had anticipated a rapid conquest of Moscow by the end of the autumn and had therefore neglected to supply the soldiers with winter clothing. At Christmas, however, from his post outside Volokolamsk, Karl looked through his binoculars to see the lights of the suburbs of Moscow – far from the warm Christmas tree lights at home.

In the north, Leningrad was besieged, and in the south, the Ukraine had been overrun as far as Rostov.

Then the tides turned. The reinforced Russian forces drove the Germans back. On Christmas Eve, 1941, the last positions of the Germans in front of Moscow were eradicated. Now, the German side lamented 600,000 injured men and 200,000 dead or missing. The senseless human sacrifices increased steadily, as the deluded German 'leader' responded to proposals by his command staff to withdraw from the frontline only with rage-filled tantrums. On 1 July 1942 the Germans once again celebrated a significant victory when they seized the fortress of Sevastopol on the Crimean Peninsula. In August, however, they began their calamitous attack on Stalingrad. There they were surrounded and trapped until well into winter and there they experienced their first truly devastating defeat. The 6th Army was encircled with 260,000 people. 170,000 men fell and 90,000 were captured, of which only 6,000 returned home after the war. If one includes Russian soldiers and civilians, over one million people lost their lives in this attack on Stalingrad. Among them, Dieter's older brother Wolfgang fought there and was never heard from again.

The defeat at Stalingrad initiated the unravelling of the German Armed Forces. After a last daring attempt to regain the battlefields on all Eastern front lines in a campaign called 'Citadelle', from 1943 onwards the German armed forces were repeatedly defeated with heavy losses. At the same time, in May of 1943, all North African territories had been lost to the Allied enemy forces, and American and British divisions had landed in southern Italy. The entry of the powerful economic giant, USA, into the war provided the turning point in the reign over the Atlantic Ocean and in the air over Europe. By increasing bombardments of major utilities and supply routes, the German armed forces grew weaker and weaker. Then, on 6 June 1944, American and British armed forces landed in Normandy on what is now known as D-Day. By the end of July, the Allies had liberated France, Belgium and the Netherlands from occupation and opened a fourth front in the West, which tied up even more German forces and resources.

So, as you can see, on 22 June 1944, as Dieter and his four companions were set in motion, there was nothing left to win. On that day, which also was the third anniversary of the German attack on the Soviet Union, the so-called 'Red Army' (the Russian army), with a force of troops never encountered before, started its decisive counter-offensive against the Centre Group of the German army. They had already beaten the Germans far back into the West. Now they rolled onwards with the united power of a total of 200 divisions consisting of ten ground armies and four air-force armies, roughly 5,000 tanks, 45,000 guns, 7,000 airplanes and 12,000 trucks to transport 25,000 tons of ammunition, diesel fuel and supplies. In four sections of the Eastern Front they squeezed the last German forces like pincers and pulverised them. By the end of June – within just one week – the Germans had been pushed back by 300 kilometres (186 miles) and the front was torn apart along a stretch of 350 kilometres (217 miles), so that a mere month later the Russian forces arrived on the border to East Prussia. The Army Group Centre had been dissolved.

The envisaged European empire under German rule of injustice, meant to last a thousand years, had instead, after only a few short years, shrunk back nearly to its original size and was now, under the grip of Allied forces, on the verge of disappearing altogether.

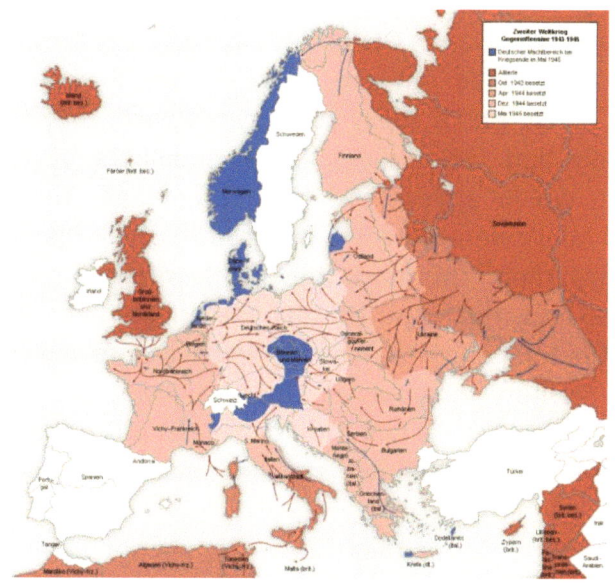

Advancing allied forces 1943-45
https://de.wikipedia.org/wiki/Deutsche_Westfront_1944/1945

Between Fronts

Unaware of the inexorable advance of the enemy against Germany from all directions, and still under the illusion of achieving fame and honor as brave soldiers for 'Führer', 'Volk' and 'Vaterland', Dieter and his companions sat in the forest and waited out the attack of the Russian fighter planes. 'Well, this is really starting out well', they thought scornfully and wondered whether members of the Resistance would appear and bring them hell. The woods around Minsk were known to be a centre of the Russian partisan movement, this much they had learned from front returnees. Also, they worried that the enemy aircraft might bomb the train and that they would have to march through hostile territory for hours to the next town. They did not know whether they would even be able to reach their squad or whether they would fall into the hands of enemy troops first.

Then, as suddenly as they came, the aircraft disappeared, and the soldiers streamed out of the woods back to the train. Our five also sprang from their hiding places in the bushes and climbed back onto the train as it started to move on. Dieter and the other three followed Hildebrandt instinctively, since he was three years older and more experienced. Hildebrandt had already been at the front, as was evident from the ugly scars on both sides of his face caused by a gunshot that had gone right through the sides of his mouth. So naturally Hildebrandt had taken the lead from the very beginning of the journey.

Soon afterwards, they arrived in Minsk, the still-occupied capital of Belarus. Nothing was yet known about the success of the Russian tanks on the nearby frontline. At the command post, the five were told that their unit was still in Bobruisk, so they took a train from Minsk and headed south.

Bobruisk lies, *nota bene,* by the Berezina River, a place that had been the epitome of utter defeat for Napoleon. This river, it seemed, would hold the same fate for Hitler, just as the Rubicon River had held for Caesar: they should never have crossed that river! [5]

Our five clueless soldiers had only gone as far as the little Belorussian village of Asipovichy. There, the train could not proceed any further, because the Russian forces had already broken through the railway line further south. Asipovichy was situated about two-thirds of the way down from Minsk to Bobruisk and thus about 90 kilometres (56 miles) south-east of Minsk. Night had fallen and the town was in turmoil, because Russian soldiers were expected, and they were known for not dealing gently with the civilian population. When our five soldiers inquired about possibilities of continuing their journey, they were given orders by the local commander to defend the town with the few other soldiers around. The 'old fox' Hildebrandt realised that this was a suicide mission. So that night, he went back to the local headquarters to protest, but the order for local defense stood. To avoid being detained, he pretended to fetch his comrades saying they still had his pay book. Previously, he had seen a train of wounded soldiers on the opposite track of the train station. Now on his way back, he made a deal with the train driver that the five ROBs could be used as armed guards for the train. In this way they managed to escape Asipovichy. They took turns on the machine gun post on the train and ended up back in Minsk. Later they learned that on that very same night of 28 June 1944, the Russian

---

[5] Caesar's crossing of the Rubicon, a small river in northern Italy, which had separated Italy from *Gallia cisalpina*, led to a civil war in the year 49 BC, marking the beginning of his downfall.

forces had driven the Germans back across the Berezina River and had taken Brobruisk. Once again, they had been incredibly lucky.

At the command post in Minsk, they were told that their unit had retreated to Slutsk, which was situated in a swampy area directly to the south at a distance again of about 90 kilometres (56 miles). They were given new marching orders to go there and soon they were travelling again like sardines in a train crowded with soldiers. And once more, they failed to reach their destination. 'Not again', growled Wöhrle, as their train came to an abrupt stop in the middle of nowhere and the call: 'Everybody leave the train' made the rounds. They were told that the journey could not continue because the enemy was nearby. This, however, was not true. This time the train could not advance further because it was out of fuel. The chaos of the collapsing front caused disorganization of the communication and supply lines. This time, the only option was to proceed on foot. So, together with the other train passengers they set out on an arduous foot march, while their gear weighing heavily on their shoulders.

After they had walked more than ten kilometres (6.2 miles), they encountered a road which crossed from the east. On it was a slow-moving stream of trucks, carriages and refugees dragging their belongings towards the west. They followed this stream and stayed overnight, cramped with several refugees and civilians in a cabin by the road. The next day, they were allowed to hop onto the trailer of a military truck, which dropped them off in Baranowice, a town southwest of Minsk. Their heavy artillery battalion had apparently pulled back from the Eastern Front by more than 190 kilometres (120 miles) within two days, which must have been quite a rushed retreat. They spent the following night in a Russian farmhouse. With a couple of fresh eggs, which were 'given' to them by the farmer's wife – who was probably terrified of the German soldiers – and with their portion of liquor, they made a kind of eggnog which was not well-received by Dieter's bowels. Nevertheless, Dieter wanted to give the peasant woman a part of his bread in gratitude, but Hildebrandt grasped his arm and snapped at him: 'You idiot, have you not noticed that there is a war going on here?' It was true that this peasant woman could easily surprise them with partisans in the middle of the night to slit their throats. The partisans were known to be as brutal as the Nazis who left captured and executed partisans hanging in the trees for days as a deterrent to resistance activity. Dieter had seen this for himself in some villages on their long march to Slutsk.

Once finally in Baranowice, they received new marching orders sending them back to Minsk! As if in a maze, they kept returning again and again to this starting point. As they arrived in Minsk for the third time, the heat was lying heavily over the city. Hardly a human soul could be found. This was the calm before the storm. They learned that Russian forces had now taken control of the railway lines from Baranowice to Minsk, thus cutting off a retreat route to the west. The city was almost completely surrounded by enemy troops. The only possible way out of Minsk ran to the northwest, in the direction of the Lithuanian capital, Vilna.

Looking for something to eat, they entered the central building of the former communist party (GPU), which had recently served as the headquarters of the SS[6]. An abruptly abandoned breakfast of half-eaten eggs was still on the table. Clearly, people had fled in a mad rush when they realised that the enemy was approaching. In the building's basement they discovered a box of soda bottles, some SS jackets

---

[6] SS = 'Schutzstaffel', literally translated to 'Protective Eschelon' was the paramilitary organisation of the Nazi party: Hitler's private army.

(which they later got rid of again) and mosquito nets. Once again, they succeeded in pulling their heads out of the sling by offering to protect a train of wounded soldiers. Quite possibly it was the very last train to leave Minsk. So they hired themselves out again on a train car with a light machine gun. Two days later, on 3 July 1944, Minsk was retaken by the Red Army and five days later, Baranowice was taken, as well. The Eastern Front was collapsing like a house of cards.

The burning University of Minsk on 3 July 1944
http://commons.wikimedia.org/wiki/File:1944_burnin
g_university_minsk_july_3rd.png

A Sign of Life for Mother

On the trip to Vilnius, the train stopped in Molodechno. The train station here had been completely bombed out by the enemy. At some point they'd heard about a food warehouse that was going to be vacated, because 'the Ivan' – which is what Russian soldiers were generally called by German troops – stood just outside the village borders. Our five comrades hurried to the warehouse, seeing the opportunity to find food supplies. They arrived there to find a crowd of citizens which stood lurking around the warehouse master who was preparing to defend the food reserves with his gun. After a brief report on the rapid advance of the enemy, the warehouse master's resistance broke and the supplies were looted in wild confusion. Dieter was able to secure cigarettes of the brand 'Austria Reggie', a bucket of honey and stuffed chocolate bars; he consumed the chocolate immediately. On the way to Vilnius with their train of wounded soldiers, they were attacked by partisans in a forest. They fired several volleys with their machine gun back into the bushes. The chocolate clumped heavily in Dieter's stomach, while his sticky hands guided the machine gun. Luckily, there were no casualties or injuries from this incident.

In Vilnius, the station was filled with refugees. In search of food, the five were able to find a truck that would bring them to a bread factory outside of town in the evening. From there a train carried them back to Vilnius train station. Soon after, their train departed via Grodno back westwards to the former Polish town Bialystok. The next connecting train from Bialystok to Volkovysk, back eastwards into Belarus, where their battalion was supposedly stationed, was to leave the following day. Dieter had enough time to rush to the post office and send about 2,000 cigarettes which he had picked up at the warehouse in Molodechno to his mother in

Karlsruhe. And indeed, they actually arrived several days later and with them they brought Dieter's mother a sign of life from at least one of her three men along with one of the most valuable currencies of the war – one could trade cigarettes for almost anything. Dieter's father Kurt was back in Sicily as ADC officer to General Rommel's army. ADCs were officers who had been decorated with war medals in the First World War and now had to keep up the morale amongst the other officers. His job was to motivate highly decorated, daring Air Force pilots – in propaganda language: 'German flying aces' – for what were then hopeless and most often deadly missions. Dieter's older brother Wolfgang, as mentioned earlier, had sent his last letter on Christmas Eve of 1942 from Stalingrad and had not been heard from since. He was meanwhile officially considered 'missing in action'.

In the meantime, on 13 July 1944, the Russian forces took Vilna. Like sand castles slipping away under the flooding waves of the sea, one place after the next fell beneath the feet of the retreating soldiers into enemy hands. Nevertheless, our five ROBs spent the night in Bialystok and reached Volkovysk by train the following morning.

Volkovysk was a key military control centre that was a major hub for the Eastern Front. For soldiers on their way to the front, this was the terminal station for the German Reich Railway and the connecting station for their final leg of the journey to the dreadful front. For returning front soldiers, this was the starting point of their dreams: to return home to their loved ones. If only Dieter and his companions could have boarded one of these Reich Railway trains and remain seated in it long enough. Then they would arrive home and be far away from all the pandemonium and away from the horror stories, told by accompanying and wounded combat soldiers who probably still could not describe the full extent of the disaster: in the previous four weeks alone an estimated 350,000 German soldiers were killed or taken prisoner.

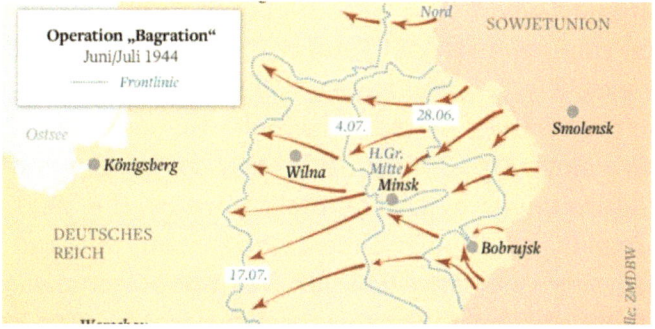

Progression of Russian military forces between
June 28th and July 17th 1944
https://www.welt.de/geschichte/zweiter-
weltkrieg/article129441875/Warum-Stalin-den-
Krieg-1944-nicht-beendete.html#cs-DWO-KU-
histKarte-WWII-Bagration-cw-Aufm-jpg.jpg

End of the Search

Dieter and his comrades remained in Volkovysk for several days. They learned nothing about the whereabouts of the military unit which they were supposed to join at the local central command station. Total chaos reigned here. No one knew exactly where the enemy had broken through, and to where the battered troops had withdrawn.

The five stayed close together in this confusion, as if in a jungle surrounded by wild beasts. Somehow, the 'old-timer' Hildebrandt found some soldiers who thought they had seen the 'fish sign', the badge worn by their troops, somewhere in the vicinity of Brest. So, they found a freight train which would bring them near the described area, close to Brest, and hopped on one of the wagons. With gestures and sounds, the Belorussian train driver made it clear to them that they needed to jump off when he sounded the train whistle three times, as they would then be near their destination. All of them dozed off as the train carried them south in a slow and steady rattle.

When the train's whistle pulled them out of their dreamless sleep, they threw their gear off the wagon and jumped off. And indeed, not far from the railway line, finally, after days in a maze, they found their troops: the heavy unit of the 'Fish' Division, the 35th Infantry Division – or what was left of it. This heavy artillery battalion, identifiable by a fish symbol, had gotten rid of all its heavy ballast on the hasty retreats from the overwhelming Russian forces. They had escaped but were armed only with light weapons: their rifles and hand guns and a few horses. The five comrades were allocated to the second Battery of Artillery Regiment 71. Sergeant Ernst Sessler, a butcher's son from Karlsruhe, immediately took the young, inexperienced compatriot from his hometown under his wing. Later, Dieter would meet him again as a cook in one of the POW camps and find a valuable friend in him. And much later – after the war – Dieter would take part in Ernst's wedding ceremony, an event which, at this point, was beyond imagination.

The badge of the 35th Infantry Division
https://de.wikipedia.org/wiki/35._Infanterie-
Division_(Wehrmacht)

During their stay in this Belarusian village somewhere not too far from Brest, the news of the assassination attempt on Hitler, on 20 July 1944, reached them. Dieter was outraged over the incident. For him, who had enjoyed his time as a squirt at the 'Jungschar', (Hitler's movement to indoctrinate the youngest with Nazi-ideology), Hitler was still an icon. Therefore, in Dieter's eyes this assassination attempt was high treason. While he and his comrades were risking their lives for their country, others at home did not support them and had tried to assassinate the 'Führer'.

Although his parents had not joined the NSDAP, the Nazi party, they had allowed him to grow up without warning him of the poisonous political background of his time. The only words which he had picked up from his father about Hitler's rise to power were: 'Hitler – this means war' or a few low, derisive words about 'that Austrian corporal', which also referred to Hitler. For Dieter, Nazi-Germany was still the perfect world of his over-protected boyhood. And thus, his faith in the 'Führer' could not be shattered so easily. Once, after the war, Dieter questioned his father about this. His father's answer was: 'I did not want to destroy your child-hood and, at the time, one wrong word or phrase reported by the innocent and clueless boys you were would have put us all in grave danger.' This demonstrates well, how ordinary, well-educated citizen of a country can be kept passive to evil behavior of their authorities by spreading misinformation and fear.

Meanwhile, Russian forces had surrounded their village near Brest, and yet again, the situation seemed hopeless. They came under heavy fire by Russian assault guns and 'Stalin's Organ': multiple rocket launchers.[7] But fortunately, a tank battalion of the well-known 'Viking' units of the armored SS-fraction[8] came to rescue them from the crossfire and allowed them to escape once again.

It was an eerily clear night on 31 July 1944 when Dieter's howitzer-stripped artillery battalion fled the village. They marched past a flock of dead sheep. Between the limp and rotting animal carcasses slain German soldiers lay with slashed-open bellies. Like a warning vision, they shone in the blue moonlight. The images haunted the young corporal on the long march of 50 to 60 kilometres (31–37 miles) to the next village and even longer, like a nightmare. Finally, the group came to a bridge over the River Bug. On the other side, it was suddenly silent. Apparently, they had left the front behind them. Here they found a stronghold of the first Battery of the Artillery Regiment 35 (with LFH 18) and temporarily joined their ranks. At last they could let go, rest, and try to forget everything for at least a short time. And indeed, in late July, the Russian offensive had come to a halt about

---

[7] Katyusha multiple rocket launchers, nicknamed 'Stalin's Organ' (*Stalin-Orgel*) by the Germans due to the weapons' visual similarity to a church organ and the sound of the rocket motors.

[8] The armoured divisions of the SS (='Schutzstaffel' see above) became infamous, because part of them guarded the 'Concentration Camps', where the mass murder on millions of humans took place, which the Nazi regime pursued considering these futile in their ill strive to build a supreme, Arian race.

25 kilometres (15.5 miles) outside Warsaw: The Red Army had developed supply problems due to their unexpected, rapid advance and, temporarily, the soldiers at the front experienced a deceptive calm.

The journey of the five ROBs in 1944 (blue arrows), progression of the Red Army (black arrows)
map:
http://www.lib.utexas.edu/about/librarymap/

The Last Battle Position

It was 14 August 1944 in the area of the town Sokolów Podlaski. On this day, another one of the mendacious propaganda speeches was preaching to them through speakers, leading the soldiers to believe they were still fighting for 'victory and fatherland' while, in reality, the frontline was breaking further and further, like tree branches under a child who climbed too high. The battalion remained in the new position for a few days and life seemed to take on a more regular rhythm. Due to his training, Dieter was initially assigned to the gunner's position on an artillery gun. Later on he served as the messenger to the commander of the battalion, Lieutenant Frübing, thus receiving more diverse responsibilities. As a consequence, he was given a horse to run errands with. Once, on a ride into the surroundings, the horse threw him off. He was alone in the woods. Thoughts about recent partisan warnings reeled through his mind. What an easy target he was! He tried his best to capture the beast, all the while cursing it under his breath. Dieter must have had a guardian angel, though, because he managed to catch the nasty nag again, although it took him quite a while.

After a few days, the order came to relocate the battery into an area about 20 kilometres (12.4 miles) east of the confluence of the Narew River into the Bug River. This was not far from the railway line from Warsaw to Bialystok and about three kilometres (1.8 miles) west of Wyszków. Regardless of war or peace, the Bug River flowed here on its usual course from west to east, dumping its water, and perhaps even the remnants of these terrible events into a bigger river and eventually into the sea.

Dieter's unit had to set up a new battery firing position on a ford over the Bug, aiming to prevent the crossing of the Russian forces camped on the southern shore. Only later did

Dieter realise that the 7th Infantry Division, (abbreviation ID), along with the 5th ID and the 35th ID were setting a trap to ambush the enemy here.

Dieter was then reinstated as a gunner and was set on the 'B'-post. This is the observer position, usually on a hill or an elevated place, from where the front and the target area could be observed from afar. In this case, it lay about five kilometres (3.1 miles) before the Bug River. On the afternoon of 24 August, he was assigned to a new post, as he was ordered to serve on the 'VB'-post, the forward observer. 'Forward' in this case meant that he was positioned much closer to the frontline and directly in his unit's line of fire. Soldiers sat near the target here, in this case the ford over the Bug, in order to watch the margin of their own artillery and to give specific coordinates to reposition the howitzers. In the event of the enemy breaking through, the very last instruction was to be 'fire on this position' – self-sacrifice.

There were three of them at the 'VB'-post: a slightly more experienced sergeant, a radio operator and Dieter. The observation trench meandered like a river in zigzags through the countryside. This was to prevent Russian fighter planes from easily shooting into it. The Bug-ford was visible at about a distance of 50 meters. The sergeant immediately instructed the greenhorn Hüllstrung: 'Do not stick your noggin out of the trench, otherwise you'll get nailed!' Dieter realised at once that he was referring to Russian snipers on the other side of the Bug who picked up anything that peeped out of the trench.

A Night at the Foremost Front

They were all very tired, so tired that their eyelids dropped every now and then. Of course, they had not had much sleep in the past days and even less to eat. Consequently, at one night Dieter fell into a really deep sleep while he was on duty. Fortunately, he soon woke himself up. He immediately felt the sudden burning heat of panic running through his body. Furtively, he looked around to see if someone had observed him while he was asleep. He was lucky; no one was around. If an officer had caught him sleeping on duty, he would have been accused of treason and been shot on the spot.

During the night of 24 August 1944, the Russian side was more active than usual. Unfortunately, the phone line from the command post had been hit by enemy fire and was out of order. The only possible way to reestablish communication with the commanding centre was to check the cable along its entire course from their trench back to the command post and to repair it right away. This had to be done very carefully so as not to get hit by a Russian sniper. To make matters worse, the dark night sky was lit up regularly by flare shots. They appeared like flashes of lightning revealing the landscape for a short time in a ghostly light. One of the three had to risk his life to fix the communication line. Dieter took the job. Each time a wheezing sound announced a rising flare, he stood frozen on the spot and waited for the darkness to envelop him again. It was far more difficult to notice a creature that didn't move. The risk of attracting attention as a rigid being standing on the spot and thus becoming a target still remained. Dieter was able to locate the damaged part of the telephone cable, to repair it and check the connections. The line worked perfectly again. Since he was close to the command station, he reported back before heading back on his reckless path to his cold trench. The post had just arrived and Dieter had received a letter from his father from Italy. He put it away to read at his post later. He could not have known then that the letter would later nearly cost him his life. At the same time, he received his salary of 100 *Reichsmarks*, a canteen filled with red wine, a tin of sardines and three magazines. Back in his trench, he gave his comrades their mail, took a sip of red wine, and read his letter. Since he was no longer on duty, he soon fell asleep.

Early in the morning he was awakened by heavy artillery fire and the sound of the engines of Russian fighter planes, the so-called 'storks', the IL2 (= Ilyushin). Clearly, the Russians were now trying to advance across the ford of the Bug. The telephone line was destroyed once again. Dieter did not dare to lift his head up to look out, but instead dug himself a 'foxhole' into the wall of the trench in an attempt to escape the machine gun fire of the IL2, which aimed downwards from both sides like dragonfly wings. With lightning speed, he scratched the earth directly in front of him, as the 'storks' from above showered the trench with bullets. His sergeant had apparently run off without a word. Later, in captivity, Dieter would meet him again on several occasions. There was nothing he could do but wait. As it slowly grew lighter with the dawn, Dieter sat perfectly still in his foxhole, took out one of the magazines and, ironically, began to read the last page with the comic strips and jokes, chuckling by himself like a child in his warm and cozy room.

Capture

With a quick glance backwards out of the trench Dieter was shocked to see a soldier running. He thought to himself: 'Is he insane? Any second now he'll be picked up by the Russian snipers'. That didn't happen, however. The soldier moved directly towards him and waved his gun barrel at him. Now Dieter recognised the Russian machine gun and the associated uniform. The soldier shouted something unintelligible to him while simultaneously moving his elbows up and down like duck wings, which most likely meant something like: 'Hands up'. Without thinking, Dieter quickly reached for his army revolver in order to surrender it obediently. He thought he'd rather throw it on the ground than have it ripped off violently together with his holster. Fortunately, the revolver did not slip right out of the holster, and Dieter had to fiddle with it. This clumsiness saved his life. Had he pulled out the gun any faster, he would have been killed instantly: the enemy soldier would have shot him in self-defense. As it happened, the Russian soldier fired only a warning shot. Dieter, however, had long abandoned any idea of defending himself after glancing along the trench. The area of the observation trench where his experienced veteran comrade had been sitting was completely obliterated. The 'storks' had been extremely effective despite the zigzag. Hesitantly, he put his hands up. A second Russian jumped down into the trench, took away his bayonet and frisked him for other weapons. Then he shouted gruffly: 'Davai, davai ...' and gave Dieter a violent blow to the flank. In this way, Dieter painfully learned his first Russian words ('Move, move ...') and as they climbed out of the trench, he saw the concentrated Russian forces crossing the river Bug through the shallow water. He was handed over to another Russian soldier, who was already pushing a few other prisoners along at gunpoint in the opposite direction of the troops, towards the Bug. Dieter recognised one of the prisoners. It was the radio operator Knies. The Russian soldier yelled at them to stop and went ahead of them through the ford with a mine detector to scan the ground for anti-tank mines. At this point, Dieter remembered that detained German officers had to prove that they had made three attempts to escape captivity. Otherwise they were suspected of being a turncoat and then were dishonored. As merely an officer in training this surely was not yet his duty, but nevertheless he suddenly had an idea. Once they were in the middle of the river, he would dive under the water and drift back with the stream into the wild until he was out of range of their guns. This, however, was easier said than done: the water was bitterly cold and the ground so treacherously muddy that it was impossible to push off from the bottom. On the contrary, as he tried to kick himself away, the mud grasped firmly at his boots, as if the river wanted to hold him back. The Russian soldier grumbled something incomprehensible and again 'Davai, davai'. Then Dieter felt a hefty blow to his belly from the rod of the mine detector, knocking the wind out of him. As he nearly passed out, he was pulled roughly back into the ranks with the other prisoners of war. He probably would never have survived this escape attempt anyway, because three kilometres further downstream even larger Russian forces were crossing the river and, even if he managed to get through that, the banks of the river on both sides had been extensively planted with anti-tank mines.

In the water, they were met by Russian soldiers who raised their rifles over their heads and shouted loudly: 'Wojnaplennis' (= 'prisoner of war') and 'Chhitler kapuutt!', which was a Russian pronunciation of the German word 'kaput' and meant 'destroyed'. One of them pointed his gun at them and then fired directly over their heads. Dieter ducked under the water and took the opportunity to quickly rip the ROB epaulettes off his uniform. He put them inside his pockets, however, instead of leaving them in the river. In shallower water another Russian soldier passed by him and grabbed at his pocket watch. Dieter in his innocence, wanted to help the soldier, so that he would not rip his jacket. But the soldier only gave him a painful blow to the ribs with his rifle butt, tore the watch off and moved on. When they arrived on the other side of the river, the radio operator Knies was beaten up and his glasses were crushed. Dieter was only pushed into the sand and spared worse treatment. Later he told us that this was most likely due to the fact that he was still a boy, or at least he looked like it. They were then driven to run into a nearby forest. At least the run helped him to get a little warmer. They passed a position of heavy mortars of the Russian artillery in a clearing. The Russian guns had a greater diameter than their German counterparts and, thus, a wider range.

From the clearing, they were led to an old farmhouse, where the Russians had apparently set up a POW collection camp. In addition, there was also a field emplacement of the 150th Russian Guards Division. Upon their arrival, the 25 new prisoners were frisked from head to toe. All useful items were taken away except for their knapsack and the clothes on their backs. Next, their hair was shaved off with sheep shears. Dieter found this very humiliating, but in reality it was merely a matter of hygiene – to protect against head lice. They were enclosed in a barn and had to sleep in the straw. This was an easy way to prevent escape attempts, because in the night the rustling of the straw would have betrayed every fugitive to the surrounding Russian guards. A Russian major with a big red star on his epaulettes immediately confiscated Dieter's soft riding boots. In exchange Dieter inherited some worn-out, far too small rubber sandals.

The officer spoke a little German and said mockingly: 'Well boy, chow many Russians you shoot?' He didn't wait for the answer, but snarled on: 'I chhave keelled chhundreds of Nazees and Fasheests!' Dieter looked at him as innocently, dumbfounded and fearful as he could and didn't dare say a word. The rubber sandals would cut cruelly into his bleeding heels on the long marches which followed. Later on, during his first night in captivity, Dieter had his first encounter with vermin. In the warm straw, they were plagued by lice each night anew. But worse than that, there were 'bigger' vermin too: on his very first night Dieter woke suddenly, as four strong arms held him down, while a third person ripped off the breeches of his leather pants. Fortunately, he was spared worse misdeeds by his fellow captives. However, there was always a brawl among the POWs when the Russian guards occasionally tossed a few rotten potatoes over the fence to the prisoners. It was every man for himself.

Prisoners of War during World War II

All of the belligerent powers in World War II were obliged to follow two internationally valid agreements with regard to prisoners of war.

The first of these was the Hague Conventions of 1899, renewed in 1907. The second was the Geneva POW Convention of 1929, which was signed by 47 countries under the aegis of the International Committee of the Red Cross (ICRC). According to Article 7 of the former, 'prisoners of war shall be treated as regards board, lodging, and clothing on the same footing as the troops of the Government who captured them.' According to the latter, humane treatment of POWs was expected, including articles governing the use of prisoners for labour: 'no prisoner of war may be employed on labour which is of an unhealthy or dangerous nature...' The Soviet Union had initially not been represented in the agreement, but finally signed it in 1941. However, they signed on the condition that the German Reich Army would also honour it.

While the German Armed Forces more or less adhered to the agreement in the west, they evaded this obligation on the Eastern Front by withholding the status of 'prisoners of war.' This was the case for about 400,000 Polish soldiers, who fell into the hands of the German Armed Forces right at the outset. They were declared 'civilian criminals' and sentenced to forced labour. Serbian prisoners of war met a similar fate in 1941. Approximately 5.7 million Soviet soldiers who were captured by the German Armed Forces from 1941 until the end of the war were not spared, either. Jews and political commissars were deliberately murdered. Others died of starvation or through countless other brutalities – everyone who was declared targets by the Nazi leadership.

Overall, only about 3.3 million Red Army soldiers survived the prisoner camps in Germany.

However, from Stalingrad until the end of the war, more and more German soldiers were being captured on all fronts. An estimated 11 million Germans in total had become POWs. In American and British camps, the German POWs, such as Dieter's Cousin Karl, were usually treated very humanely and according to the cited agreements. Consequently, a majority of them survived.

In Russia, German POWs met a different fate. They were treated no better than their Russian counterparts were treated in German captivity. On 23 February 1942, Stalin issued the following order: 'The Red Army is to take German officers who surrender as prisoners of war and spare their lives.' Nevertheless, of the approximately 3.1 million German POWs in the Soviet Union only about 1.9 million were documented to have returned to their homeland by 1956. The rest had died or remain missing. Especially after 1944, the number of Germans taken prisoner increased so massively that the Soviet Army Command ran into supply problems, making the situation for the POWs considerably worse. There was a lack of food, clothing, heating fuel and medical supplies.

According to S. Karner, the mortality rate of the German POWs in Russia in 1943 was 52.5 per cent. Most of them succumbed on long, strenuous marches or in the camps to starvation, the bitter cold, or infectious diseases such as tuberculosis, dysentery, typhoid and others. The leadership of the camps was under the command of the GUPVI, the Administration for Affairs of Prisoners of War and Internees with the previously established Gulag, which led Stalin's notorious camps for political prisoners, the GUPVI was subordinated to the NKVD, the People's Commissariat of Internal Affairs of the USSR. The GUPVI was founded in the first months of the war, on 19 September 1939, with the introduction of the new Russian rules for the treatment of POWs, and was established with the help of the Gulag. Thus, initially the Gulag was responsible for training, selection, storage, organisation and the like. Although in the wake of Operation 'Barbarossa', the first few Russian camps had indeed been overrun by the Germans, later in the war their numbers grew to nearly 5,000. Furthermore, there were not only camps for German soldiers, but also camps for Russian soldiers who returned from German captivity. These were generally looked upon as collaborators and traitors by the Red Army and usually sentenced to ten years in a labour camp. The last Russian POW camp was closed in 1956.

German POWs on their march through Belarus
in July 1944
Source: picture-alliance / akg-images/akg-images

The Interrogation

The day after his arrest, Dieter and the new prisoners were individually called in for interrogation by the Russian captain. He wanted to know exactly where the guns of Dieter's battery were located, so that they could bomb them. This may have been one reason they had not obliterated Dieter's part of the defence trench with bombs the night before: they wanted to get their hands on German soldiers for information.

The Russian officer sat at a wooden table on which lay a piece of wood. 'Thiiis I will beeeat on your chheaad kappuuutt,' shouted the angry officer with dreadfully long emphasis on 'this', 'beat', 'head' and the last syllable of 'kaput' as he looked fiercely at Dieter through a pair of glasses – consisting of one oval and one square glass – and he slammed the log on the wooden table to reinforce his threat. The loud blow startled Dieter, but he tried not to show his terror by the slightest move, not even of his eyelids. The interrogator pushed a wrinkled, dirty map towards Dieter. Dieter was afraid of being shot for giving a wrong answer, but he also didn't want to reveal his comrades' base to the enemy. So, he hurried to grasp the map and pretended to study it with complete attention. He did not have to fake fear, as he was actually frightened to death. He deliberately held the map upside down. After a seemingly thorough study of the map, he pointed with conviction to (an obviously incorrect) point, which he claimed with certainty, was the position of the gun battery. Shortly afterwards he was sent back to his fellow prisoners. The radio operator Knies whispered to him: 'Did you tell them anything?' Dieter shook his head. It was increasingly easy for comrades to become enemies if they suspected you were a traitor.

In the afternoon, the interrogation continued. An army jeep came to a halt with mud spraying from its tires and two people jumped out of it. One was wearing a parade uniform. Dieter suspected that it must have been a Polit-Officer. The other wore a so-called *Gymnastiorka*, a red shirt, which sagged under the belt and was typically worn by communist party members. This man was apparently able to speak German. He seemed to have the task of interrogating all the POWs once again, strictly adhering to the *Geneva Convention*. So, he started out by asking for names, ranks and troops at stake:

'What is your name?' – 'Hüllstrung'

'First name?' – 'Dieter'

'Where are you from?' – 'Karlsruhe'

He gave Dieter an astonished look: 'From Karlsruhe?!'

'Why, do you know Karlsruhe, by any chance?' It escaped Dieter's lips half suspiciously, half hopefully.

'Yes!'- came the abrupt answer.

'How, for God's sake, could someone on the Russian side possibly know Karlsruhe?', thought Dieter and asked: 'But you are not German, are you?' –

'Of course, I am, and most likely a better one than you!', the other one replied harshly. Dieter ignored this and asked: 'What do you know about Karlsruhe?'

The interrogation seemed to reverse itself, so that the interviewer became the respondent and answered tersely: '*Blumenstrasse*'. (Flower Street)

Dieter was beside himself, but was trying not to show it. *Blumenstrasse* was intimately familiar to him. The official and private residence of the Evangelical Bishop Bender was on *Blumenstrasse*. Dieter's older brother, Wolfgang, had tutored the bishop's son and had fallen in love with the bishop's daughter Gertrude. Prior to enrollment to military service Wolfgang had even secretly been engaged to Ger-

trude. Dieter had then taken over the tutoring job from his brother. And so, without considering the consequences, Dieter said 'I used to visit the corner house regularly ...'
'Really, whom did you visit?'
'Bishop Bender.'
'How is he doing then?', asked the man, as if they were two passengers chatting on a train.
Dieter was speechless.

Here was obviously a communist, who, due to his ideology – his Marxist worldview – had no belief in God and the church, but somehow this man actually knew Bishop Bender!
As the conversation continued, Dieter discovered that this man was a German named Matthäus Klein. He was seven years older than Dieter, had grown up near Wertheim, studied theology (!) and had worked as a vicar at the Evangelical Church in Baden. He was close friends with the Bishop's oldest son. As a soldier stationed in the Crimea, he defected (probably following capture) and claimed to be a communist. He joined the National Committee for a Free Germany (*NKFD*) and ascended to the position of Front Proxy.
In the post-war years, Dieter learned that after the fall of Berlin, this Matthäus Klein, along with members of the future leadership of the GDR (among them Pieck, Grotewohl, Ulbricht) had been flown from Moscow to Berlin on the first plane. He was later said to have become a professor of Marxism and Leninism at the University of Jena.
Dieter now implored Klein to help him get home, because his brother was already missing in action and his mother was all alone. Klein simply said: 'You will get through it.' With that, the interrogation was over.
As he was guided back a short path through the woods to the other captives by a Russian soldier, who pushed every now and then his barrel into Dieter's ribs in distrust, he grew unwary of his incautious outing about the common back-

ground back home towards this Matthäus Klein. Maybe this new convert from the Christian belief to Marxism wouldn't want to have a captive near him, who could point at him and instigate distrust in his new 'Russian friends' by unravelling the former connection of Matthäus Klein to the leader of the Evangelical church in Baden? Maybe this would motivate this traitor to get rid of Dieter. Dieter's thoughts over-whelmed him with fear and horror: 'What if this Klein will send me to a prison camp in Siberia?' Dieter had heard ru-mors about prisoner camps of the Russians in this arctic re-gion, where it was even colder than here and where death was certain. His mother would lose yet another son. Tears filled his eyes. As he sensed once more a sharp pain in his right flank by the Russian soldier's barrel, which unknowingly hit bruises from yesterday's blows during Dieter's captiva-tion, it suddenly came to his mind: 'What if Klein has already ordered this Russian soldier to shoot me here in the woods on the way back? This guy behind me can pretend to have prevented an escape attempt'. Dieter shortly turned his head and glimpsed into the eyes of a very young solder, merely older than he himself, that immediately waved with his gun barrel and shouted something ending with 'dawai, dawai!' Then they arrived at the other captives.

The National Committee for a Free Germany (NKFD)

In July 1943 at a conference with exiled German communists in Krasnogorsk near Moscow, Stalin created the National Committee for a Free Germany. Its goal was to recruit Germans for the fight against the Nazi regime and for the communist cause. For this they were seeking to engage German intellectuals with high public esteem. The first Chairman was the then renowned German writer Erich Weinert (1890–1953). Leaflets, loudspeaker announcements, a weekly newspaper and the radio programme 'Free Germany' encouraged German citizens to revolt against Hitler and urged the German soldiers to defect.

Among the other leaders of the NKFD were Wilhelm Pieck and Walter Ulbricht, who would later take over the political leadership of the Soviet-occupied zone and even later still, govern the new German Democratic Republic (GDR), which after the war was founded within the borders of the Soviet-occupied Zone of Germany as the communist counterpart to the Federal Republic of Germany (FRG), the free democratic republic founded on the three other post-war zones in Germany, the French, the British and the American zones. Both post-war German Republics were also referred to as 'East-' and 'West-Germany' and were reunified in 1989 after East-Germany's citizen overcame and tore down the Soviet-built fences and death-strips separating both countries as well as the wall, which separated the capital Berlin into East and West and encircled the Western part.

Two months after the emergence of the NKFD, the League of German Officers (*Bund Deutscher Offiziere*, or *BDO*) was founded. The main task of the BDO was to deliver propaganda aimed at the German armed forces. A number of officers held as Soviet prisoners of war eventually joined the BDO, the most prominent of them being Field-Marshal (*General-*

feldmarschall) F. Paulus, who had been the head of the beaten German Armed Forces in Stalingrad. On 11 September 1943 the BDO merged with the NKFD.

The NKFD was especially active in their attempts to recruit deserters among the POWs, promising them 'anti-fascist' schooling and an 'easier' life in prison. Apparently Matthäus Klein had succumbed to this courting by the NKFD, and now Dieter should be convinced to do the same.

Offer to Defect

Every morning prisoners had to rush to line up for their roll call in their tattered clothing. They had to place themselves in lines like in the army and had to count themselves by each yelling the count he would reach up from his neighbour. This had to be complete before moving on to their work. It could often go on for quite a while, frequently because the numbers didn't fit, either because some prisoners hadn't come back from their deadly work in the woods or because the Russian in charge was so drunk that he would mix up the numbers. Half freezing, half dozing, Dieter had quickly learned to just stay calm and not raise any attention from the camp guards, who could get angry from counting over and over again.

One morning there was a sudden announcement: 'Chhiil-strung to the guard!' This rarely meant anything good for the summoned prisoners: they often returned having been beaten up, or sometimes they never returned at all. Dieter had to muster all his courage to move up towards the guard. To his surprise, however, he was brought to see Matthäus Klein again, who simply asked him: 'Do you still want to return home?'

'Yes!' Dieter answered.

'Hmm... Your father writes *very* interesting letters!' Klein responded knowingly.

Dieter froze in terror. He had heard that Russians took letters sent to and from POWs, printed them into propaganda leaflets and airdropped them over Germany to weaken the resolve of the German people. This caused sometimes trouble with the Nazis for the captives' families. Dieter realised that the letter he had received from his father on the day before his capture had been taken from him by the Russians. He could imagine such a leaflet printed with a quote from his father's letter: 'Captain Hüllstrung writes to his son: if the Americans manage to keep their toehold, this war is over!'

He implored Klein, 'Please don't do this to my family!'

Klein simply asked, 'Were you a Party member?'

Dieter answered that he was immediately made an officer's candidate, without having to apply for NSDAP party membership.

Klein continued, 'Were you ever in Warsaw?'

'I only passed through it on the train.'

'That's good enough.'

Klein made it clear to Dieter that he could avoid a lengthy imprisonment if he decided to work for the Red Army. 'We will take you to Warsaw. There you will carry out a task and come back in two weeks.' It was an offer to defect. He was to parachute into Warsaw and spy for the Russians.

Dieter asked to think it over for 15 minutes and this was granted to him. In desperation he turned to an experienced sergeant from Sudetenland, who listened to his story and said: 'Consider this: if you take this offer now, you will pay for it later. You are getting a "loan" now, which you *will* have to pay back in one form or another!'

Dieter returned to Klein and refused the offer, saying 'My father is an officer. I can't spy for the Red Army. What should I do?'

Klein responded that there were many things he could do. He could even work in the POW library. Then, cynically, he simply wished Dieter 'a good time in captivity' and sent him away.

Dieter never saw him again. Nevertheless, after the war, Dieter noticed that Klein had apparently never passed on his incriminating letter.

Prisoner Relocation

Several days later Dieter, along with 30–40 other prisoners, was taken from the farm stall which had served as a temporary POW camp and marched to Brest-Litovsk. Dieter and several of his fellow prisoners were suffering from severe belly cramps and diarrhea due to the horrible food and the missing cooking hygiene. On their way they spent the night in Minsk-Mazowieki cooped up in a tiny room. It was so cramped that they could not even lie down and had to sleep sitting up leaning onto each other. 'Even sardines have more space in their tiny cans', was Dieter's impression. And the diarrhea epidemic did not make things better.

The next day, they met infuriated Belarusian farmers on the way who tried to attack them with scythes aiming to lynch them. For once, the prisoners were relieved to have their guards who held the farmers at bay with raised weapons.

They also once crossed a battlefield where numerous fallen soldiers lay seriously disfigured and half-decayed. As with the previous images from the spooky, nightly walk across the field with maimed sheep and soldiers, Dieter would never be able to erase these images from his mind. The war had left a hideous imprint on Dieter's soul, which would reappear in nightmares even decades after the war, as his wife Elisabeth would witness later on in his life. She would wake up in the middle of the night by his feet running under the sheets, while he would pant and grasp for air in fear of some virtual hunters.

The prisoners stayed in a small POW camp near Lukow for a few days. It was there that they heard that the war was over in Finland, as they were mocked as losers. Dieter had begun to learn the Cyrillic (Russian) alphabet, which came easily to him because of his knowledge of ancient Greek, which has similar characters. He also tried to improve his spoken Russian.

In the meantime, the Russian bedbugs enjoyed the endless food supply, which the prisoners' veins offered to them. In the dark, these nocturnal bloodsuckers crawled out of the cracks in the woodwork, up the walls and then let themselves fall from the ceiling onto their victims. Therefore, the lights were left on in the barracks at night whenever possible so that these photophobic pests would stay hidden in their crevices. A Russian doctor took pity on Dieter, who had scratched himself bloody, due to the dozens of itchy bedbug bites. She gave him an unidentifiable and smelly, but very effective, salve against the itching.[9]

While the nights didn't grant much force restoring sleep, the days continued with the exhausting march in the merciless summer heat. Dieter still wore the tight, rubber sandals that sliced into his heels. Those who survived these long marches – later often referred to as 'death marches' – finally arrived at the first larger POW camp at Brest, Belarus.

There, for the first time, Dieter had to wait in the long food lines for the 'Panje-Wagon' carrying bread rations and soup. The POWs were used to store provisions in the Citadel. A small Russian officer who supervised them gloated in German, referring to the – long since disused and made illegal – lyrics of the German National Anthem: 'Deijtschland, Deijtschland iiber alles? Ha! Jetzt: alles iiber Deijtschland!' ('Germany, Germany above all? Ha! Now it's everything above Germany!'). Dieter often tried to seek contact with him, asking him irrelevant, naïve questions and cautiously trying to learn some more Russian from him, but unfortunately, they only stayed there for a few days and were then transported by train to Minsk.

---

[9] The salve possibly contained urine. Urea, a main composite of urine, is still used in creams and lotions today for its anti-itching properties.

Forest Camp 168 Minsk

In October 1944, Dieter and his fellow prisoners arrived at the Forest Camp 168 Minsk, where they would remain throughout the winter. This was a large, former German POW camp in which the roles had now been reversed: the Russians were the guards and the Germans the prisoners.

Approximately 15,000 men lived in the camp. Like everywhere else, mornings started early here with their line-ups for a long working day in teams of 15–20 men and repeated count-offs. Their meals consisted of a cup of weak tea with 10 grams of sugar in the mornings, a pint of soup with a 1-pound loaf of bread at midday and another pint of soup in the evenings. Fish soup was nothing more than a weak broth with fish flavouring and a few overcooked fish bones. Pea soup was water with pea flavouring and a few hard peas inside. An old tin nailed to a broomstick served as a soup ladle. Other old empty tin cans served as bowls and other dishes. Dieter received an old 'Oskar Meier' can, which was probably left behind by the German predecessors. To keep from burning his fingers, he wove a rusty wire around the can to serve as a handle.

The bread was made out of so-called 'potato-*Klitsch*' (a type of runny potato flour); it was very watery and lay like a brick in one's stomach. They received one loaf of bread per day for five men and had to divide it up evenly. The crusts were the best part and highly prized. Every now and then they were also given 'Kasha', a type of bland porridge made from buckwheat seeds; for the prisoners this felt like the equivalent of a Sunday feast.

They were also regularly given a ration of tobacco crumbs which they rolled in newspaper and called '*Machorka Stalks*'. The cigarettes diffused their hunger and made the stench of decaying life that pervaded the camp like a plague somewhat bearable. They rarely had the opportunity to wash themselves. Most of the prisoners became chain-smokers. In desperation, some even rolled peat moss into cigarettes.

The prisoners had to work for their meagre meals. Dieter was assigned to a squad charged with peat digging and cutting. Every day after roll call and the obligatory count-off, they were forced to pull sleds through deep snow about 8 kilometres (about 8 miles) into the forest. The path was cumbersome and the aluminum wire cables with which they were harnessed to the sleds cut deep into their shoulders. In the forest, they had to dig up peat which was needed to heat the barracks. Digging into the frozen ground was nearly impossible. Every day, exhausted prisoners were literally worked to death. If the Russian guards, with their weapons and dogs, didn't shoot them, they simply left the collapsed prisoners behind without pity, knowing full well that they had no chance of escaping or surviving a night outside in the Russian winter, where either the relentless frost or the wolves would catch them, before any guard would have to spoil his energies.

According to the accounts of Roland Altmann who, like Dieter, spent Christmas 1944 in the Forest Camp at Minsk, 500–800 men were housed in each barracks. Dieter was assigned to Barrack III in the Barrack-Complex I-III, which was surrounded by two barbed wire fences. Even at temperatures of -25°C (-13°F) they still had to perform their roll call every morning, which lasted sometimes for hours. In rows of five they had to line up and count off: 'Dawai, dawai, po pjat, po pjat! Ras, dwa, tri, schitiri, pjat, sches, sjem …'.

In the beginning, the POWs were dressed only in their thin German army uniforms, which were not made to cope with the Russian winter. It was only much later that they received a Russian quilted jacket: the 'Fufaika'. Also, only about every

30th prisoner had sturdy shoes. The rest had to use straw and strips of burlap which they wrapped around their feet.[10]

On Christmas Eve, of all days, there was no flour delivery, as R. Altmann recollects in his written memories. Instead of their daily bread, the prisoners were given only their watery soup with a few grains of hulled wheat floating in it. They referred to these as 'Calf teeth' and it seemed as though the soup was smiling at them mockingly. At the next morning's roll call several prisoners swayed and more of them than usual fell over in exhaustion. The rest scrambled dejectedly back to the barracks.

It wasn't until three weeks later, on the 15 January 1945, that they had another bread delivery. Quite unexpectedly they even received an extra loaf, by way of compensation. However, many of the starving prisoners wolfed down the bread in one sitting and paid for it soon afterwards with excruciating abdominal cramps and vomiting.

One can assume, that their stomachs and intestines had shrunk from lack of food and nourishment, and that their salivary glands had dried out, so that this sudden huge amount of 'food' completely overwhelmed their digestive systems. Other prisoners were wiser and saved some of their rations of bread, but they had to be extremely careful not to have it stolen by the other inmates.[11]

The best opportunity for thieves was the monthly trip to the sauna. In small groups they had to hand over all their clothes, were allowed to wash themselves with a bit of soap and cold water and then they were sent naked and half frozen into the heat of the sauna. This was to get rid of body

---

[10] House of the History of the Federal Republic of Germany (Editor): *Kriegsgefangene*. Droste Verlag, Düsseldorf, 1995.

[11] Altmann R.: *In a Windowless Time: Soviet Captivity 1944–1949; A Survivor Reports*. LIT Verlag Berlin-Hamburg-Münster, 2000.

lice which were known to carry the dreaded spotted fever. The clothing was also heated – and judging by the smell – also chemically treated against the beasts. They had to hide their belongings very deviously if they ever wanted to see them again. Prisoners sewed hidden double pockets or double seams into their cloths in order to hide private belongings. They also had to be extremely careful about being pushed into the sauna with certain fellow inmates, for the sauna was a common place for demeaning physical assaults. Sadly, there appeared to be no way to eradicate this type of 'vermin'.

Insomnia, Frostbite and Hunger Swelling

Insomnia also plagued Dieter in captivity. The prisoners slept in 3-level bunks, each only 50 cm (19.6 in) wide. The top bunks were favoured, since these were warmest. They had other advantages as well, as the reader will later discover. Sleep could be disturbed in many ways. For example, if someone turned around in his sleep, it caused a domino effect; the whole row had to turn as well. The bunkmate snoring, his rolling around in his sleep, his trips to the latrine as well as fleas, bedbugs and thieves all chiselled away at Dieter's hard-earned night's rest. Worst of all, however, were the gruesome war images, which appeared especially often at night and, no matter how exhausted he was, kept him wide awake.

Modern psychologists have a name for this pathological phenomenon: post-traumatic stress disorder. Even in 1987, 42 years after World War II, they were able to diagnose this condition in 50 per cent of American POWs who had been held captive in the Pacific theatre during World War II.[12] Further, even 50 years after the war, a third of the cases of British POWs held captive in the Far East showed persisting symptoms.[13] It can only still be speculated at why people experience this horrid type of psychological self-torture after a traumatising experience. Perhaps it is a defence mechanism intended to protect the affected person from the paralyzing shock of a similar experience in future and help strengthen their will to survive. In a misguided form, howev-

---

[12] Goldstein G., 'Survivors of Imprisonment in the Pacific Theatre During World War II'. *American Journal of Psychiatry* 1987; 144:1210.

[13] Hughes J., 'Former Prisoners of War Show Symptoms'; *British Medical Journal* 1994;309:873.

er, this can also lead to an obsession with the trauma and increase the desire for vengeance.

In addition to the ghastly mental images, which regularly deprived Dieter of sleep and the exhaustion during the day, the intense cold and lack of food also pushed his body to the limit.

The human body is actually designed to live in a tropical climate and is inadequately equipped to cope with the cold. In order for the body to process food, bring nutrients to the muscles, fight illness and send messages from the body to the brain and commands from the brain to the body, it needs a constant temperature of around 37°C (98.6°F) in the blood and organs. As soon as the nerves in the brainstem experience an extreme loss of warmth, for instance due to the scant clothing of the POWs during the Russian winter, they 'batten down the hatches', so to speak. This means that the brain restricts blood-flow to the extremities – the fingers, toes and nose, which are hopelessly exposed to the cold – and tries to maintain the life-saving warmth for the inner organs. Without sufficient circulation to the extremities, however, the nerves become numb, the blood becomes thicker and the small blood vessels become water-permeable. In this way, the skin can no longer offer protection against injuries: blisters appear, slowly open and the skin dies. The results are chilblains and frostbite.

When sacrificing the extremities is still not enough to keep the body's core temperature up, Plan B is initiated: the body's muscles receive the command to create warmth through constant shivering. This only works, however, as long as the body temperature does not drop below 33°C – after that the muscles have lost too much strength to continue. Slow paralysis occurs and the body's core temperature plummets. At about 30°C (86°F) the person loses consciousness, the heartbeat slows down and at around 27°C (80.6°F) it stops completely.[14]

Long before that, however, a person's mental abilities are severely impaired. With only a drop of 1°C (33.8°F) brain metabolism is reduced by 5 per cent and the electrical nerve impulses slow down. This causes a decline in mental ability, memory, body coordination, moods, reaction time, and the ability to concentrate. Prisoners become withdrawn and apathetic.

In addition to sleep deprivation and the constant cold, the third dark force attacking Dieter's will to live and resistance to death was malnutrition. Over time, Dieter's legs began to swell and the swelling continued upwards. One of his fellow prisoners, who had already been imprisoned for a longer period, warned Dieter. He explained to him: 'This is due to the lack of food. I have seen other prisoners die from it as soon as the water reached the heart.'

And indeed, when the body can no longer get enough energy from food to keep its organs, such as the brain, muscles heart, liver and kidneys functioning, it first mobilises its rapidly available glucose reserves in the liver and muscles. Within a few days, these stores are depleted and the body looks for the next source of energy stored in the system, which is fat. So, it immediately starts to convert fats into energy. Fat has almost double the amount of energy than sugar and proteins but in people who are not obese, these reserves only hold out for two or three weeks, even though their body has simultaneously gone into energy-saving mode, which shuts off or at least reduces functions not absolutely necessary for survival: decreased reaction time, immune response, tissue repair (wound healing), sexual function and much more. For

---

[14] Kamler K., *Surviving the Extremes*. Penguin Books, 2004.

these reasons, it is not recommended to use extreme fasting as a weight-loss method.

If starvation continues, for example through the calorie-deficient diet in a POW camp, the body is forced to tap into its last reserves: its own basic body structuring component, the protein. Protein makes up about a third of a person's body weight, but it also forms the structural element of muscles, heart and brain: basically every organ. This means that the body starts to burn itself: as if you lit your car on fire to keep it going. Sooner or later, there is nothing left.

In Dieter's case, the long nutritional deficiency which had already started on his odyssey to the Front was now reaching a critical point: his extreme protein deficiency was causing hunger swelling.

In healthy people, transported proteins hold water within the bloodstream, preventing it from leaking into their body tissue by something called oncotic pressure*. As blood protein falls to abnormally low levels, water leaks from your circulation into your tissue, which leads to the body literally drowning in its own fluids. Gravity causes this fluid to collect in the legs in the form of swelling (oedema). This is one of the first visible signs, but at the same time, fluid slowly fills the body's cavities such as the abdomen, the chest and the pericardium, until the inner organs begin to fail. The results: pulmonary oedema, liver and kidney failure, pericardial effusion and finally cardiac arrest and death.

Dieter's fellow prisoners gave him some advice: 'You have to put your legs up during the night, so that the water can drain off.' And as predicted, by hanging his legs in wire slings attached to the frame of the bunk above at night, the progression of the swelling actually seemed to slow down. This, however, made sleeping all the more difficult because he needed to empty his bladder several times a night. It dawned on Dieter that he would never survive a second winter of this bitter cold and lack of food.

'There has to be a way out of this miserable situation', Dieter thought as he slowly drifted off to sleep after one of his freezing nightly trips to the latrine. But this seemed so absolutely hopeless, absolutely out of reach...

Quilted Jacket (*Fufaika*) and equipment
of a German returnee from captivity in
Russia after 1945

A Life-Saving Idea

... Dieter's physics teacher sent him into the room they called the 'witches' kitchen' to prepare the next lesson. Only Dieter and his friend, Meinrad, were allowed to enter the room. They were to set up a piece of equipment for an experiment in the next physics lesson. There were stacks of uncountable, bizarre pieces of technical equipment everywhere. Meinrad pointed to a single everyday object, a Black Forest clock, which hung on the wall. Dieter was not interested in that, and continued to search the crowded room for the required equipment. His friend called: 'But look here, the mechanism is open, the clock only has one hand and it functions without a pendulum...' Dieter looked up and noticed that in place of the pendulum there was a vertical shaft that projected out of the wooden clockwork and that from the crossbeam there hung a lead ball on each side...

The wake-up call startled Dieter and pulled him back into the horrid reality of his captivity. He had been dreaming about his school days with his best friend Meinrad. Slowly he realised that in a few minutes he would be forced again to dig up peat in the merciless winter cold of the Russian forest. Later he wrote about this time saying: 'One could almost predict how long the oil in (one's own) lamp would hold out.'[15]

It was well known that the Russians needed craftsmen to rebuild their cities. They were referred to simply as 'specialists'. A former physical education teacher from Dieter's barracks pretended to be a carpenter and was transferred by

---

[15] Hüllstrung D., 'Small Cause – Huge Effect', Essay from the 1980s for a high school newspaper.

the Russians to the specialists. The specialists represented, in a way, the 'high society' of the POW camp. They were not sent out on peat digging detail, but rather had their own warm workshops and received better food rations. The communist idea of a classless society didn't even hold up within a POW camp.

Dieter's dream gave him an idea for passing himself off as a 'specialist.' He remembered the Black Forest clock that had hung in the physics preparation room very well. He had managed to figure out and memorise the basic functions of a clock from its simple mechanics. So, Dieter went to speak to the oldest in his barracks: the butcher Tebe from Iserlohn. Everyone feared him because he was brutal, dumb and devious. Most likely this was the reason the Russians chose him to be in charge of the barracks. The meanest and nastiest prisoners were promoted to guards, given privileges, and they made use of their power. It was best to stay far away from them. Dieter went to Tebe anyway and offered to make a clock for the barracks, since he, as Dieter mentioned incidentally, was a clockmaker from the Black Forest.

Tebe believed this lie and secretly reported it to the Russians. And so it happened that at roll call the next morning, on 1 March 1945, Dieter was called out of the group and was no longer marched off to dig peat. Instead he was sent to the 'specialists' in the camp's carpentry workshop with the task to build a clock.

There he first crouched, hungry and frozen, in front of the stove and began to realise the possible consequences of his shirking. 'Just don't let anyone notice,' he told himself. 'Otherwise you will be known as a liar and given even harder work than peat digging!' Suddenly he noticed a small bowl of Kasha (buckwheat porridge) which had been placed next to him, as if by an angel. He had no idea who had given it to him, but at that point he realised that even here, under the most deplorable conditions and among some of the most disagreeable people, there was good to be found – and he fortified himself with this Kasha. Later he learned that carpenters always received extra portions because they made dishes, cooking spoons and the like for the kitchen and privately for the prisoner guards. Dieter desperately wanted to learn all of this.

It didn't take long for the other carpenters to realise that this young boy didn't have a clue about anything and had certainly never gone through an apprenticeship as a craftsman. They could, however, clearly use an apprentice who, after a second glance, made a rather clever impression.

When he found out that Dieter, like himself, also came from Karlsruhe, one of the older carpenters immediately took the boy under his wing, like a hen would her chick. And so, little by little, Dieter learned carpentry skills and met some very sturdy craftsmen. People from the same region stuck together here in captivity. Dieter continued to meet people from Baden or even Karlsruhe, such as the former Karlsruhe lantern lighter, Erich Ruppental, whom Dieter would meet in the military hospital. These people helped Dieter and with them, he was able to share his longing for home. And so Dieter learned a lesson, which overthrew the wronged ideology of Social Darwinism and Fascism: To be good or evil was not a question of race or nationality, but of character.

At the same time, Dieter worked meticulously on his Black Forest clock for the barracks so as not to be exposed as a fraud. He needed an entire two months to carve the pins, pegs, frames, grooves, hands, and gear, to cut and glue the housing to find a chain and weights and – unlike in his dream – a pendulum set at the correct height. Incidentally, his creation was hung up in the barracks on 8 May 1945: the day the war officially ended. It seemed as though the clock was there to count the hours and minutes, which the inmates in the barracks had to wait for, until their time of peace and freedom.

Word of a watchmaker in the camp spread like wildfire among the Russian guards and more and more of them secretly approached Dieter and asked him to repair this or that watch, which they had stolen from the prisoners. The guards didn't seem to mind that Dieter's barracks clock didn't keep exact time or that he often needed a long time to make the repairs. They all had more than enough time as prisoners and guards.

In spite of all the misfortunes of captivity, fate dealt Dieter two lucky hands with his transfer to the carpentry workshop. Firstly, as he now worked in the workshops inside the prisoner camp, Dieter was certainly spared imminent death from cold and exhaustion while peat digging in the woods. Secondly, as he was simultaneously transferred to Barracks XI which was located in the craftsmen complex in a separately fenced-in area of the camp, he escaped spotted fever. As to say, shortly after his transfer, spotted fever broke out in his former barracks, carried by new prisoners brought in from the Crimean Peninsula. The entire building was put under quarantine and, after everyone inside had died, it was unceremoniously burned to the ground.

When Dieter realised that his feigned 'specialisation' had saved his life – twice over! –, he worked tirelessly to acquire new skills. One of his fellow prisoners was able to use his drawing abilities as a 'side job', paid in bread or cigarettes. He later painted Dieter's portrait. This inspired Dieter to hire himself out as a calligrapher. Because of his humanistic education, he made good progress in Russian and quickly learned the Cyrillic alphabet. He began to carve names and inscriptions into wood and made himself indispensable in the carpentry workshop. In addition, he was able to emboss inlays in self-made tobacco cans or other tin cans with a compass, which he had received from a generous guard.

To keep the compass and other useful tools from being stolen in the sauna or at night, he sewed hidden pockets into the seams of his knapsack and in the inseam of his trouser legs.

In time, he was used by his comrades not only for carpentry but for all sorts of work, even outside of the camp. He learned woodcutting, sawing, planing and wood-shaving, sanding, gluing, grouting and much more. He even learned the art of making casks and barrels from a cooper, which would prove useful to him some time later. At the same time he was trained for a few risky smuggling jobs. His first smuggling attempt with a fish under his shirt was a complete flop, however. The commandant saw right through him as he tried to pass the guard. He pulled the fish from under Dieter's shirt and, roaring with laughter, slapped him repeatedly across the face with it. Apparently, he had expected to find much worse under Dieter's shirt.

Together with the winemaker Adolf Heuber from Bahlingen/Kaiserstuhl, who was assigned to the metalworkers, Dieter later smuggled potatoes into the camp inside an old oven pipe. He hid several other useful things under a girder from a horse-carriage. Adolf Heuber also survived his captivity, returned to Bahlingen and cultivated his vineyards. Many years after the war, Dieter's then six-member family were able to help with many grape harvests.

In the Hospital

Dieter was not spared from disease, however. One night he woke up uncomfortably to find that the bunkmate who slept on bare metal wires above him had diarrhoea. This was one of the more disgusting disadvantages to having a lower bunk. Shortly thereafter, Dieter was put in the military hospital for diarrhoea.

The camp military hospital was a solid, stone building which had been built by the predecessors and stood in the middle of the northern camp wall near the water tower. Since, according to the official record, prisoners were not allowed to die in the camp, a 'hospital' was built just outside the camp but directly adjacent to the camp hospital's wall. There was a directly connecting door to this outer hospital where dying was 'permitted'. Soon every patient in the camp hospital learned of this door and it made everyone shudder to think who was to be transferred to the other side. It was synonymous with Charon's raft ride across the River Styx – there was no coming back.[16]

As he laid suffering in the hospital, the fleas tormented him more and more. To get rid of them, one usually rolled up his underwear during a run to the freezing cold toilet where it was too cold for the fleas so that they looked for warmth elsewhere; however, the pests always returned. With so much time on his hands, Dieter practised new ways to rid himself of this plague: he trapped them. When he saw a flea, he drew a wet circle around it with his saliva, which the fleas avoided. They couldn't escape, and Dieter then picked them off and squished them. In his flea-accompanied boredom,

---

[16] In Greek mythology the dead were taken across the River Styx by the ferryman Charon into the Underworld.

Dieter eventually began to write poetry. He wrote about everything that plagued him, from the fleas to the hunger (translated into English):

'The Ballad of the flea: I am completely alone with myself / into the dawn, dreams gone, / something is crawling on my leg / and begins to bore into me. // Do you think you can trick me, / think you can plague me day and night / eking out your living? / Pest, just wait, I will hunt you! // But as it is in life: / as soon as you have found one, / you make your move and miss, / and the enemy is long gone. // Will Artemis not bring me luck? / Will I get no rest tonight? / Oh yes! I have him by the neck, / destiny now be fulfilled. // Leniency will do no good here, / gentleness has no purpose here / between my fingertips / his robber's life has fled. // And now I can lay to rest my head! / Already Morpheus nods gently to me, / there seems to be something moving – / Ow, a bite! Gone is my rest! // Finished my dream, wide awake my senses! / Will this torture never subside? / Whatever I do and begin, / I must forever kill the fleas! // So, I surrender to the silence / (Nature is right and just), / that it is simply God's will / an eye for an eye, blood for blood. // The breeding fleas want to bite, / then look for safety in their flight, / I must break their backs, / or I will never rest tonight! // Yes, great and small, / there will always be the survival fight, / always thorns on Roses, / and the weaker ones will die!'

To kill time, he even translated the poem into Latin (unfortunately only the beginning was passed down):

'Solum sum, solissime, / sine somnium dormire /
… / inter ossa subito / cerpet quid et vult purgire.
/ … / Credidisti me turbare / …'

One should not be deceived, however, by Dieter's lovely poetic endeavours; here in the camp hospital his situation was just as dire as if he had been under fire at the foremost front. When the body is so emaciated, diarrhoea can lead to death in a very short time.

In the American Civil War, for example, only 19 per cent of the Yankees died directly on the battlefield and only 12 per cent died from battle wounds. By far the highest percentage, eventually 63 per cent, died from disease. The most common of these deaths were caused by an insufficient and/or deficient diet, especially vitamin deficiencies such as scurvy and pellagra, by infectious diseases, especially pneumonia and dysentery and by combinations of both.

After the introduction of vaccinations, antibiotics and antiseptic operations, the mortality rate from disease in the US Army in World War II dropped by a factor of 10 as compared to the rate during the Civil War. The treatment options in the Russian POW camps during World War II were, however, terribly deficient. There were no vaccinations or antiseptic operations available and a very scarce supply of antibiotics. Therefore, the medical care of POWs in Dieter's camp in Russia was rather comparable to the conditions in the Civil War in 1860 than to those in American POW Camps during World War II.[17]

According to J. Geller, a Polish prisoner who worked as a camp doctor in a Russian labour camp from 1940–1941, there were hardly any antibiotics or antiseptics available even at the beginning of the war. Doctors could do little

---

[17] Gilchrist M., *Disease and Infection in the American Civil War*. The American Biology Teacher 1998;60(4):258-62.

more than frequently wash the patient, give them warmth, a better diet, rest and moral support. In cases of pneumonia they could only inject camphor oil. For scurvy, which is caused by a vitamin C deficiency and leads to increased susceptibility for infections, muscle atrophy, as well as various skin and gum diseases, they could only prescribe rosehip. For pellagra, which is caused by a vitamin B deficiency and leads to red skin lesions, diarrhoea, depression and mental confusion, they would apply or inject nicotine acid.[18]

One can read many accounts which state that hunger and disease were commonplace in Russian POW camps. From shipwrecks, we know that prolonged starvation leads to a narrowing of perception and leads to obsessive thoughts that revolve constantly around food. While the body slows down and goes into power-saving mode, even sexual desire is shut off. In this way the only source of pleasure is channelled into thoughts of food. Starving castaways describe the most succulent recipes and envision the finest banquets, which serve as a sort of stomach-masturbation.[19]

The same thing happened with POWs. Dieter expressed these thoughts quite harmlessly in verse:

> *'Raging hunger in my belly, / lying powerless in the ward, / this, it seems I must endure, / since not normal is my stool // I would have liked to hide this fact, / but my situation time reveals. / There is no enjoyment at this time, / as, for a while, I get no meals. // Although the doctor, scholar, he / claims that this ordeal will pass, / –*

---

[18] Geller J., *Prisoner Doctor in a Soviet Labour Camp 1940–41*. British Medical Journal 1989;299:1601-4.
[19] Reported in: Philbrick N., *In the Heart of the Sea*. HarperCollins Publishers, London 2000.

*he says, as if to comfort me / I will get better
with this fast. // But isn't that the same, / as if
you wish my guts to lame? / Rather a corpse the
other way, / than here so starved and depraved!'*

He also wrote a Latin version of this one (though again only
the beginning here):

*'Venter vanus / non corpori sanus: / famus pus
cor meum regit / cubo sine vi et spe. / Sic fortuna
me coegit / breve dictum: diarrhoe. / ... '*

The medics in the camp hospital were also German POWs.
One of these, Herbert Reschke, who would become a chemistry professor in Berlin after the war, could simply not allow
this young poet to waste away. Secretly, he gave Dieter a
daily spoonful of cod liver oil from a barrel that he had found
in the basement. With this additional help, Dieter was slowly
able to recover from his diarrhoea and regain his strength.[20]

Since Dieter's health was improving, he was expected to
start 'raboti' (work) again – his only purpose here – and so
he was assigned to provide 'room service' in the hospital.
This meant cleaning the ward and the latrine. Once, while
doing his chores, he had to go through the infamous 'last
door' to the 'outer' hospital and pass through a room filled
with dysentery patients. He witnessed a gruesome sight
there. The floor – flooded with bloody diarrhoea excrements
– was bridged over with planks. The deplorable sight of the
emaciated patients lying there without sheets, barely
clothed on the planks of the beds, left an unshakable chill in
Dieter. He had been very close to ending up in this room like
those poor fellows.

---

[20] The liver not only detoxifies the blood, but at the same time stores
vital nutrients and vitamins, especially vitamin A, D, E and K.

Later still, he also had to run errands for the kitchen. As he went out to get steaming water for the hospital kitchen one day, he met a cross-eyed fellow prisoner, who silently and arduously was pushing a type of flatbed wagon in front of him. As he approached, Dieter could see that it was piled high with barely covered emaciated corpses, some with partially gnawed-off limbs. These had come from the 'outer' hospital and were dumped in mass graves outside the camp. How easily it could have been him lying on that wagon! Not for the first and not for the last time, Dieter thanked God. A Psalm from his childhood came to him:

'Yea, though I walk through the valley of the shadow of death, I will fear no evil: for thou art with me; thy rod and thy staff they comfort me.'[21]

Slowly Dieter's relationship towards the Bible also began to change and he started to read it in a new way. He occasionally borrowed it from a bunkmate from Stuttgart, who regularly read the New Testament. Dieter increasingly began to see how it described the timeless human condition in dealings with happiness and misery and that it was not just filled with dates, names and historical events of over 2,000 years ago which he had had to memorize for his confirmation. No – to him the Bible now read as a promise, a promise of comfort and security, of the return home and of a better life, if only by holding on to the good and especially by seeing and searching the good in people and situations, refusing to be corrupted by the inhumane deeds and conditions surrounding him.

---

[21] The Bible, Psalm 23, Verse 4.

Peat-Digging Detail near Minsk

Several weeks later at yet another morning roll call, around the end of May/beginning of June 1945, just as Dieter's life in the camp began to take on its usual and, with the early summer temperatures, bearable routine, he was assigned to a small group of prisoners. They were told to pack their things to be transferred to another camp. The words 'foot march' and 'peat-digging detail' were also mentioned. Dieter had a sick feeling in the pit of his stomach. So far, he had survived the Eastern Front, the Russian winter and dysentery and had found a useful activity as a carpenter's apprentice and even made a few friends. Now he was expected to walk through the valley of deathly foot marches and peat digging all over again? Could he survive all that? Would he ever make it back home? The war was long over: why weren't they sent home again?

He stood with around 200–250 men, ready to march. They hadn't been able to say goodbye to hardly anyone. At least his buddy, Franz Isi, was coming along. And off they went on a 20–25 kilometre (12–15 mile) march, accompanied by armed Russian guards.

When they came upon a deserted, half-destroyed farm, the whole squad stopped. Dieter and Franz were called out of the line and taken to the workshop on the farm. They were ordered to work here as carpenters and to re-build the farm. A soldier on patrol would come by every day to check on their progress. If they tried to escape, they would be shot.

In spite of all of his earlier fears and dread, this almost felt like summer camp for Dieter. They worked more-or-less regular hours, were given their watery soup and bread without having to wait in line, slept on straw rather than in narrow rows on planks or wire, and there was no counting and waiting each morning at roll call, no being hitched to sled or wagon, and no barrack nights. Even their relationship with the patrols relaxed a little more each day.

On the very first day, they found a field of potatoes behind the house, from which they often managed to steal a few. To keep the patrol guard from giving them trouble about the potatoes, Dieter promised to make him a wooden bucket. But Dieter made certain that it was not completely water-tight, because he did not want to collaborate with the ene-my too much. A few days later, the outraged guard returned with the bowl to complain. Dieter answered with his very effective, feigned naiveté and zeal. He promised to seal the bowl. And so he returned it a few days later with visible ma-chine marks in a few places, but still leaky. And once again he got by with his POW mantra: 'Just play the dumb, clumsy little boy so as not to attract any attention.'
Unfortunately, the 'summer holiday' did not last very long. Franz and Dieter were soon taken away from their 'summer camp' and transferred to a different POW camp.

POW Camp 13 Minsk

In the autumn of 1945 Dieter was interned at Camp 13 near Minsk. This is where he would spend the longest time: nearly two years – until late summer 1947.

All in all, Dieter's camp life took on a similar routine to the life he had known at the forest camp: morning roll call, work, watery soup, some bread, sugar and tobacco, and cramped sleeping quarters. Once, it was so cramped that they could only fall asleep lying head to foot and foot to head rolled up together. When Dieter couldn't sleep, he studied the stars and had his comrades explain the constellations of the northern hemisphere to him. The stars and the New Testament continually gave him the comforting feeling that he was still connected to home, because he knew that his mother, too, was sleeping under these same stars at night and that she was praying for him.

Nearly every month now he wrote a card to his parents in which he downplayed the realities of his captivity and mostly spoke of his future and seeing them again. It is not completely clear what exactly motivated his misrepresentations. Perhaps he truly wanted to ease his mother's worry or perhaps he was afraid that if he wrote the truth, that his card would never be delivered. It is also possible that he was ordered by the camp leaders to write such accounts. In any event, the careful, beautiful penmanship showed that Dieter still believed in some sort of order and that he invested a great deal of love in these signs of life that he sent home. He numbered each card, some of which still exist, since his mother fortunately kept them after the war.

At some point around mid-1946, they began to receive wages for their work, which they could supplement with side jobs. This meant that within the camp, cigarettes were no longer the only currency used. Now there was money to exchange.

For a short time, thanks to his well-kept dividers, which was proof of him being a specialist, Dieter was once again assigned to the carpenter's workshop. Then he was transferred to the construction brigade. Their leader was a Mr. Aurel. They constructed settlements for the workers of the Minsk automobile plant, where they also assembled trucks for the USA. Dieter's job was to remove each and every nail and board from the shipment crates with the auto parts. The slats then had to be planed to make floorboards and then were laid.

Once, the prisoners had to unpack a crate of new sewing machines from Germany. This was obviously some of the Russian's spoils of war. The prisoners, however, secretly threw out the shuttles from each of the machines, so that 'the enemy' would not be able to use them. This was how life went on, year by year in captivity, with no end in sight.

Classical Theatre in Captivity

Over time, Dieter craved more and more for some type of meaningful, intellectual activity. Although he always found some time to quietly and secretly reflect on the Bible, he longed for a creative exchange with like-minded people.

Fortunately, there was already a long established theatre group in the camp. The Russians had allowed it, probably because they hoped it would improve morale and the prisoners' willingness to work. They even allowed German classics to be played, as long as these did not conflict too much with the communist ideology. Founder and director of the group was one Lutz Deisenroth, who had worked at the Düsseldorf Theatre before the war. The group was already complete, however, and it was well-known that they were not accepting any new members. Dieter realised, however, that the group lacked a prompter. Thus, he still managed to find a way to be accepted into the group by suggesting to Lutz Deisenroth and his comrades that he could work as a prompter. At first, they laughed at his suggestion, because they only had one single book available from which everyone had to learn their lines and there was neither a proper place nor lighting near the stage for a prompter to work, so they replied scornfully: 'How do you want to prompt in the darkness?'.

Dieter did not let this stop him and said, 'Well, I could memorise the entire play each time and whisper the lines from underneath the wooden floor.' As he said it, he tried not to imagine what it was like to crawl around on the damp and dark ground under the stage. With that, he impressed the lads enough and got his chance to get accepted into the group. After he proved himself with the first play, *The Sisters* by Chekhov, Dieter had the job and was allowed to memorise other plays. Later in life he was still able to recite from memory long passages from many German classics: from Schiller's *Intrigue and Love* and *William Tell* to Goethe's *Faust*.

One day the troupe needed someone to play the role of Louise in Schiller's *The Robbers*. Up to that point, all of the female roles had been played by a female German air force major: an aristocrat. She was in the camp with her husband and both belonged to the theatre group. But one day this lady was transferred to an officer's camp and certainly left a gap in the theatre group. There was no other female around to fill the gap.

The camp's barber therefore cleverly weaved a few old un-ravelled ropes into a wig to be worn by the man chosen to play the role of Louise. All of the actors tried on the wig and, just for fun, they put it on Dieter's head, too. Suddenly, everyone exclaimed 'Hurrah!' The young, late-blooming Dieter, who still had never needed to shave, seemed born for this role. With a good sense of humour and a great deal of enthusiasm, Dieter agreed and became Louise. The downside of this was that he had suddenly become a transvestite celebrity on stage, which attracted more than a few lonely hearts. On several occasions he had to reject some of his comrades who wanted to flirt with him. Nevertheless, Dieter continued to accept and play the various female roles.

Transfer to the Donets Basin

In the late summer of 1947, part of the team was transferred to the Donets Basin on the Black Sea in southern Russia to work in the coal mines there. After a lengthy journey
on a train behind a tedious, snorting steam engine, they arrived in the Camp Novwyi Ekonomitscheskoje, which lay to
the south of Donetsk and about 70 kilometres (43 miles)
north of Zdanov.

Dieter didn't really know if this change would hold more
advantages or disadvantages. On the one hand, he had
heard about the difficult working conditions in the infamous
coal mines from other prisoners who had been transferred
from there. And he would be even further away from his
home. But would he ever return home at all? On the other
hand, he could certainly expect a milder winter in the south.
After more and more believable rumours of prisoners actually being sent home had circulated through the camp, the
Russian Camp Commander announced one morning that, in
the following year as an incentive, the 'best worker' would
be freed from captivity. Dieter therefore started to become
a bit more hopeful.

Fortunately, Dieter didn't have to work in the mines, where
workers were regularly buried in cave-ins or drowned from
flash floods. Dieter was again assigned to the *Stoljarnaja*
Brigade, the carpentry workshop. In addition to the prisoners, Russian men and women also worked in the mines and
lived in barracks near the camp. It was shocking to see
women among the miners. From the constant kneeling in
the mine shafts, these women could no longer properly ex-
tend their legs and had to crawl around on their knees. Evenings were often filled with their beautiful, melancholy singing and made the prisoners homesick.

In January 1948, Dieter was appointed to the machinery room, which afterwards he remembered as being the (relatively) best time in his captivity, although he never spoke much about it. This was probably due to the fact that the year had fewer hardships and so passed by more quickly than others.

Return of German POWs from Russia

Although the western Allies (USA, France and England) had already released their 1.1 million German POWs in 1946, the USSR was more interested in keeping their approximately 3 million POWs as labourers for the reconstruction of the Soviet Union. At the Moscow Conference of Foreign Ministers in April 1947, Russian Foreign Minister Molotov announced that over a million POWs had already been released and that only 890,000 POWs were still being held. Under pressure by the western powers, he agreed to release all of these by 1948. In fact, as early as 1945, Russian leaders had indeed made arrangements to repatriate German soldiers. This, however, only applied to the wounded, sick and disabled. The selections were made based on regular medical check-ups by the POW camp doctors. The prisoners were assigned to one of four categories of working ability. The weakest were released.[22]

To keep the working motivation and morale among the POWs high, however, the prisoners were told that only the best workers would be chosen for release. After all the wounded and disabled had been released, the Russians carried out phony trials and summarily convicted all able-bodied POWs of being 'war criminals', sentencing them to six years in general labour camps. In this way, Russia was no longer holding any 'prisoners of war', but only 'war criminals' who were required to work off their sentences. Thus, after the war, the Soviet Union was able to deny the existence of POWs in their custody without strictly lying. In the end, it required several further foreign minister conferences, increasing pressure from the international community and a

---

[22] Ordinances 3921 from 4 July 1945 und 9343 from 13 August 1945 of the State Defence Committee (GOKO).

visit by the German Chancellor Konrad Adenauer in 1955 to Moscow, before the last prisoners of war held in Russia were finally released in 1956.[23]

[23] Wittfeld T., *German Prisoners of War in the Soviet Union*, Hauptseminararbeit (essay), Heinrich-Heine-University Düsseldorf, 2001, http://www.hausarbeiten.de/e-book/100697/.

The Decision to Starve

In the autumn of 1948, Dieter again had to pack up his things and climb onto a truck alongside several other prisoners headed to yet another camp in the Donets Basin: the Nowvy Gorlovka camp. This camp held about 1,500 prisoners. Here Dieter had to work on a log frame saw. In October he sent his 32nd card home. In cramped writing, but still unbrokenly fine calligraphy, he gave his parents hope and said he weighed 71kgs (156lbs) at a height of 178cm (5'10"). For the first time he was able to sew a photo onto his card. Possibly, in light of the international negotiations, the Russians wanted to make a humanitarian impression.[24]

They were repeatedly given medical check-ups, referred to as 'the pickings', and each were assigned again into one of four working-categories: for heavy work (I), moderate work (II), light (III) and very light work (IV).[25]

The Russian examiners tossed their prisoner ID cards onto one of four piles, whereby the stack with the class IV–workers (very light work) was always the smallest. Dieter observed that prisoners who were boasted as the 'best workers' at morning roll call were never the ones who actually had been 'graded' for the most difficult work, but rather always the ones whose papers had been tossed on the smallest stack. Dieter then realised that the Russians were only pretending to release the best workers, but in reality only let the sickest and weakest go, the very ones they needed the least.

---

[24] Hüllstrung D., Correspondence card Nr. XXXII from camp 7242 USSR.
[25] Karner S., 1995, S. 140: from the Guidelines 28/7309 of the NKVD for the Economic Use of POWs for the Reconstruction of the USSR.

On New Year's Eve 1948 Dieter finally come to the decision to starve himself out of captivity. It had become clear to him that the Russians would never release him early from prison when he was one of the best workers. They would never keep their promise to release the best workers, as these were the ones they needed the most. He would only be released if he were in among the sick and weak, only able to do 'very light work' – if his papers were tossed onto the smallest pile.

He wanted to implement his plan in the summer. One of his countrymen and fellow prisoners, Ernst Sässler, must have been released around that time, because Dieter mentioned him in the card he wrote to his parents in March:

'Your response to my Christmas card made me very happy. [...] We can talk more about my future career plans; some of which you have surely already heard about from Ernst. [...] you could not find a better source of information anywhere. For me, here, he was more than just fellow countryman and comrade. [...].[26]

In February 1949, Dieter was once again transferred by truck to another camp: Camp Gorlovka. It was about the same size as the previous camp, and he was sent to work at the Palace of Culture in Gorlovka. Among other tasks, the prisoners had to free the bombed palace of rubble and debris. They often found the remains of people who had been killed in the bombing raids. They also had to clear away the half-decayed and horribly disfigured bodies.

At this point, Dieter began his starvation period, which was easier said than done. He had recently learned that hunger-strikers were placed in prison camps and force-fed: and there were plenty of spies among his fellow inmates who hoped to win the favour of the guards by betraying their

[26] Hüllstrung D., Correspondence card Nr. XXXVII from camp 7242 USSR.

comrades. But that didn't always end so well for the snitches. A spy from the neighbouring barracks had hanged himself after being discovered and ostracised by his comrades. Dieter knew well enough however that it was not only snitches, but also the typical symptoms of starvation that could betray him.

Dr. Ancel Keys from the University of Minnesota wanted to learn more about the consequences of starvation in concentration camps and created a simulation of this situation with volunteers in 1945. From this he observed and noted down the following signs: lethargy, emotional, sleep and balance problems, concentration, coordination and loss of libido, energy and listlessness, oedema, skin discolouration and eye paralysis. He attributed this mainly to nervous and endocrine dysfunction as a result of lack of protein, vitamins and trace elements.[27]

Dieter knew all too well from experience that hunger oedema (swelling) could easily betray him. Perhaps he also knew about the typical skin and mucous membrane bleeding or the dark stains around the eyes, which were the result of vitamin deficiencies. He certainly also knew that these deficiencies could lead to death.

He somehow figured out that he must manage to starve himself while at the same time get just the right amount of protein and vitamins. In any event, he knew he had to proceed very cautiously and carefully with his secret hunger-strike so as neither to be caught nor to die. He had to find a way to make it look like he was eating regularly, while at the same time making the food disappear so as to give the impression of being sick but not starving.

---

[27] Reported in: Philbrick N., *In the Heart of the Sea*. HarperCollins Publishers London, 2000.

He finally mustered up all his courage and shared his secret plan with his best friend, who agreed to secretly eat Dieter's bread rations. Dieter would give up eating bread, but continue to eat other foods which contained protein and vitamins in very small amounts. Soon Dieter got into the habit of walking through the camp with a loaf of bread under his arm whistling cheerfully, so that everyone could see that he had things to eat. When summer came, he strengthened that impression by taking the money he earned from his work and side jobs and spending it on extra bread. He continued to give his daily rations of soup to his friend.

In early summer, he worked in construction. Dieter saw this as an opportunity to see the camp doctor. He was already quite emaciated. Before the appointment, he intentionally let himself get sunburned. He also knew that black tea could have a fever-sustaining effect. He therefore spent the entire day chewing on his tea leaves. In the evening he was able to go to the doctor with a fever. Dieter answered her questions as openly and as disinterestedly as he could. Then the doctor listened through a stethoscope and tapped with her fingers on his chest, after which she began to draw blue crosses on parts of his chest with chalk. Dieter overheard as she instructed the medics to organise a transport to the city for X-rays. She obviously suspected that he had pulmonary tuberculosis, which was dreaded for being highly contagious and fatal.

During the ride into town Dieter's heart pounded in his throat. He was afraid that somehow the X-ray machine would show that he was faking it. His anxiety grew as he sat in the waiting room of the hospital. Then one of the attendants came out and told them to return to the camp, because the X-ray machine was 'kappuutt'. So, they returned to the camp empty-handed and Dieter sighed with relief at this stroke of luck.

Since they suspected him of having pulmonary tuberculosis, he was immediately moved into the camp sanatorium, where he received special rations and was given 'cupping' treatments. For cupping, rounded glass ball-shaped cups, known as 'Banki', were heated with burning grease paper and placed on the marked places of the skin. The cooling subsequently created a strong vacuum which caused the cup to suck tightly against the skin. It is believed that the increased blood flow through the tissues below the vacuum is responsible for the healing effects of this ancient therapeutic technique. Effective or not, cupping also adhered to the highest Hippocratic oath: *nil nocere,* 'to do no harm', which was quite important to Dieter. The Russian doctors were friendly and Dieter did not see them as enemies. After several weeks, he was released, but he was no longer assigned to the construction brigade. Instead he was sent to the road work detail, where he had to shovel sand from the back of a truck on the road.

A few days later, there was another 'picking': the examinations to divide up the prisoners according to their ability to work. After the usual check-up, Dieter waited for his friend, who had been standing behind him in line. As his friend came out, Dieter knew from his facial expression that something good had happened. His friend professed that he had seen where Dieter's papers had been placed: on the pile for 'very light work' – the pile for candidates who should be released.

Release from Captivity

It was Pentecost Sunday 1949, in mid-June, at morning roll call when Dieter was again assigned to a special work detail. He was ordered to unload a wagon of sand with a few men. For one whole day, they shovelled together in the sweltering summer heat. Then, the same evening at roll call the guard announced once again that some of the 'best workers' were to be sent home early. As usual among the prisoners of war, unrest broke out as the nearly 50 names were read out – those who would not have to go to work tomorrow. At long last, Dieter's name was called!

The next day, Whit Monday, he received new clothes, was told to pack his bags and, along with the other lucky prisoners, was loaded into a truck at the camp gate.

He could not quite believe his luck just yet because there had been rumours of released prisoners who had ended up in Siberian prison camps or in front of a firing squad. For the moment, however, they were taken to the quarantine camp Makejevka. They spent two quiet weeks in this camp for former regime opponents and captured SS soldiers[28], until they were placed in an open freight train via Kiev and Dnepropetrovsk and arrived in Brest-Litovsk. For a few hours Dieter once again found himself in the place where his 5-year imprisonment had begun. Then, after one last extensive frisking, the prisoners were transferred to the 'Europe-track'. From there they travelled further by train to Frankfurt/Oder.

---

[28] Members of the 'Schutzstaffel' (*protective echelon*), 'SS' for short: the paramilitary organisation of the Nazi party.

Another returnee, Horst Messer, who had a similar trip to Dieter's, described the return trip in this way:
'All the people from this school, including the German teachers, were loaded into cattle cars at the station in [...]. The ride went from Riga over Vilnius, Kiev to Brest (border). A final check by the Russians, then it continued in Polish trains (standard gauge) with no more locked doors, via Warsaw to Frankfurt/Oder. Spirits were high. In Frankfurt, we arrived at the transit camp, were registered by the Germans and received by party officials, who hoped to recruit us into the party leadership for the building up of East Germany.'[29]

The closer Dieter came to home, the less he was able to believe that the nightmare had now actually come to a late, but happy ending. In Frankfurt /Oder, he found himself on German soil for the first time in so many years. In the Horn-barracks he finally held his Russian discharge papers in his hands and was given the opportunity to send a four-word telegram home. He sent the following: 'Wait Ulm Arrival Dieter'. Perhaps they hadn't understood the hidden insinuations of his imminent return on his last monthly postcard – the last of around forty postcards – from the 'labour camps' (Remember? Officially there were no more POWs in Russia). On his last card dated 22 May 1949 he had sewn on a picture of a dove and written about interesting girls waiting at home and noted at the end: 'The anticipation is the best part.' (see page 101). Because he was afraid that his mother's heart would stop with the joy of receiving this card, he sent the telegram to his father's workplace, the dairy centre in Karlsruhe, in the hope that his father would sensitively deliver the news to his mother. His father evidently did not share Diet-

[29] Messer H., ‚Erlebnisbericht von Herbert Horst Messer aus Woduhnkeim/Ostpreußen', (experience report)
http://www.jendreyzik.de/weblog/messer/horst_messer.htm.

er's concerns. Upon receiving the message, he asked a driver to take him home immediately, charged into the house with the telegram in his hand, and joyfully announced Dieter's return, whereupon his wife, Josephine Hüllstrung, fainted.

Hüllstrung D., Correspondence card No. XXXIX from camp 7242 USSR

The Return Home

For the first time in many years Dieter sat on a public train with civilian population. It was shocking to see the destruction in Germany. He remembered its proud and unspoiled appearance which had impressed him so as he was sent off to war. At every station he now saw women holding up photos of their missing husbands and sons for the passengers in the passing train, hoping for news of their loved ones. In addition to settlers in war-torn clothes moving from the occupied territories in the East, bringing their meagre belongings to the West, there were also many foreigners. Dieter respectfully avoided these since, as victors, they now called the shots in the country. The journey continued from Cottbus to Leipzig where they were divided into groups according to their destinations. Dieter's destination was Hof. They made a stop at Plauen where they stayed the night at the castle Oelsnitz. Again, they had to show their upper arms. The Russians wanted to be sure that they were not setting any former SS soldiers free and therefore wanted to check for the characteristic blood-group tattoo. Dieter had a childhood scar under his left arm which he feared might be taken for a removed SS tattoo. But they let him pass.

The next day the train brought them to Hirschberg. Suddenly the train stopped on the open tracks, but before the old images of the train stop during an air raid on his way to the Front and lingering doubts of peace and freedom could rise up inside him, they were instructed to transfer to another train with West German markings that was standing on the track just ahead of them. This train brought him to Hof, where at last the long pent up tensions and silent hopes were released as unrestrained jubilation, that he finally had left the Russian controlled territories und with this captivity.

He was not a prisoner of war anymore, but a returning soldier on his way home, yes finally, four years after the war had ended.

With feelings of elation the journey continued via Regensburg to Ulm. From the station they were taken to the barracks in Ulm, where his father was waiting for him with the car. His mother had not come; she wanted to prepare a feast for the reception at home. But she had handed his father a welcome note to pass on to Dieter:

'My dear Darling-Little-Lamb!
What joy! You're back home! How we all thank our God! I would have liked to come along to pick you up, but Father thought it was best that I should now 'kill the fattened calf.' I hope you are not disappointed that we have to wait a few more hours to see each other.
Deepest heartfelt greetings and kisses,
Your Mother

And if the heart has a hundred gates as Thebes has – then let the joy come through all of the hundred doors!'
Hüllstrung J., 'Welcome Note to Dieter' of 27 June 1949

Finally, back in his beloved Karlsruhe, the modest German way of life felt like heaven on earth to Dieter. Here, too, however, he had to undergo a sort of 'picking'. A medical examination by the military authorities classified him as '100 per cent war-disabled' and from August 1949 he received a disabled war veteran's pension of DM 90 per month (DM = Deutsche Mark, the German postwar currency until the introduction of the Euro between 1999 and 2002).
At first, he 'set up camp' on the, for him lavishly royal, couch in his parents' living room. The Hüllstrungs had been obligated to share their four-bedroom apartment of 100 m^2 with

a family of eleven Bohemian refugees. Dieter's father rushed to the registration office the next day for a request to reassign their refugee family to another location. The office initially showed little sympathy for the war returnees ('Russian captivity was your own bad luck'). However, after a few months, Dieter was able to move into his own bedroom again.

Although he had long since signed up for the university while on home leave in 1944, he did not yet begin with the first semester of his chemistry studies. Instead Dieter followed a job offer at the carpenter Kuppinger & Jarolinek in Karlsruhe. His time in captivity had not been entirely useless for him, because in just two months, from September to November 1949, Dieter had completed his carpenter apprentice-examination piece, a three-door wardrobe. At the final examination to evaluate the piece, the carpentry master opened the closet door and slammed it with a powerful swing. Simply linked by joints and glue, the cabinet was completely airtight, and the slamming door was slowed by the compression of the air inside. The door swung quietly and, without a sound, slid into the frame. With this, he had passed the exam, and Dieter's new technical skills were officially recognised.

In the winter semester of 1949 Dieter finally began to follow his long-cherished dream of becoming a chemist and began his studies at the Technical University of Karlsruhe. In autumn 1950, he joined the Palato-Sinapia fraternity and began to catch up on much of his lost youth with new friends, parties, dances, music and sports. In the winter semester of 1957/58 Dieter completed his studies with the title *Doctor rerum naturalium*. He was hired into a lifelong career as a chemical researcher for the Bayer Corporation in Leverkusen, dedicating his free time to thanking God for his life by singing in the church choir and tutoring the children of the neighbourhood in Latin and chemistry. He also taught Sunday School to several generations of youth in order to give them a sound foundation which would help them overcome even the worst possible times in life.

After the long march through the desert, he had finally reached his promised land. The odyssey was over.

> **Heimkehrer**
>
> **Karlsruhe-Stadt.** Breuer Ernst, geb. 3. 8. 18, Lager 7242/18 Gorlowka; Hagsfeld, Schwetzinger Str. 34; Huellstrung Dieter, geb. 19. 2. 25, Lager 7242/3 Gorlowka; Karlsruhe, Hirschstr. 95; Wachner Kurt, geb. 23. 6. 29, Lager 2041 Gorki, Karlsruhe, Adlersr. 13.
>
> 27. 6. 1949

Returnees

Karlsruhe-City. Breuer Ernst, born 3.8.18, Camp 7242/18 Gorlowka; Hagsfeld, Schwetzinger Str. 34; Huellstrung Dieter, born 19.2.25, Camp 7242/3 Gorlowka; Karlsruhe, Hirschstr. 95; Wachner, Kurt, born 23.6.29, Camp 2041 Gorki, Karlsruhe, Adlerstr. 13.

Notice: *Baden Latest News* from 27 June 1949